REMEMBER WHEN A BOOK COULD SCARE YOU?

"A deeply cinematic and original read that will
scare the pants off you."

**Dark with twists, a uniquely gifted boy falls into a
dangerous cat-and-mouse game with the arrival of a
monstrous protector...searching for something of the past.**

Neurodivergent, young Dwight Skinner considers his mental
challenges to be a superpower, but it's a pure bloodline that will
put him in danger. When a tragic event brings a mysterious
Romani neighbor, Mr. Mortimer, out of seclusion and into the
Skinner family's lives, Dwight and his emotionally overloaded
mother find an unsuspecting protector in this dark whisperer.
Death and horrific secrets trail the unfolding life of Mr.
Mortimer's past, and questions soon arise as to who has the more
sinister of intentions, Dwight or the "Gypsy" he unconditionally
trusts. *The whispers have the answer.*

**Whispers of a Gypsy brings fear back to horror and
psychological suspense the way we remember classic Stephen
King and Thomas Harris novels, while adding Patten's
trademark penchant for hair-raising twists and capturing
some similarities to current horror favorites of Alma Katsu,
Stephen Graham Jones, and Gabino Iglesias.**

D1236706

Whispers of a GYPSY

J.T. PATTEN

HELBOUND
CHICAGO

First edition cover copyright 2022 by J.T. Patten

Cover artist François Vaillancourt

Interior Design by Renee Rocco

HELBOUND Productions first edition eBook

November 2022 ISBN 979-8-9873005-0-3

HELBOUND Productions first edition trade paperback

November 2022 ISBN 979-8-9873005-1-0

A Warning to the Reader

This book contains subject material including violent and graphic scenes and descriptions that some readers may find disturbing or triggering. Content also includes contextual negative descriptions and/or mistreatment of people or cultures. These stereotypes were wrong then and wrong now. Rather than remove the content, we want to acknowledge its harmful impact, learn from it and spark conversation to create a more inclusive future for society.

Preface

During the Holocaust, 70% of the Romani population in Nazi-occupied Europe was exterminated.

Na bister 500,000.

"Life is so generous a giver, but we, judging its gifts by their covering, cast them away as ugly or heavy or hard. Remove the covering, and you will find beneath it a living splendor, woven of love, by wisdom with power."
—Fra Giovanni

"Evil is unspectacular and always human, and shares our bed and eats at our own table."
—W.H. Auden

Chapter One

September 2022
Skokie, Illinois

T rue evil entered young Dwight Skinner's life with a little *nosh narrishkeit*, though his parents warned the children about food choking risks. Grandparents, to the contrary, test the frayed rope of perilous acts by the weight of their own ticking time, to steal precious moments from those around them. Yitzhak Skinner was no exception, as he encouraged his two grandsons to have a little fun with food to satisfy his own whims.

He pressed a long, translucent finger to his thin, cracked lips, which broke into an impish smile. "It'll be *our* little secret," he said to Dwight and Aaron.

Deception was the heart of the Skinners' safety for three generations. Secrets, their mistress.

The boys were eager to indulge their zayde's whims of unsanctioned mischief when their parents were out of eyesight or earshot. This was a perfect opportunity.

A simple hanging kitchen table sconce glowed a dirty amber and cast an audience of macabre shadows backdropped by the creeping rumble of distant thunder. Under it, eighty-six-year-old Yitzhak leaned far back in the creaky chair and opened his jaws wide, a silver wire attaching a yellowed dental bridge in his gaped mouth. He absently tongued the wire, tempting a resurgence of memory...a time never spoken of...memories of survival.

Ten-year-old-Aaron tossed the grape at his zayde's mouth. Yitzhak followed the fruit, tracking its launch above his chrome-rimmed spectacles, eyes darting, head swaying. It flew in a perfect arch and landed on point.

Success! Yitzhak flung his arms in the air as he chomped on the grape with a tight smile.

The young boys clapped and cheered.

"Goal! Dwight, you're up," he coaxed his twelve-year-old grandson. "And after, I'll throw into each of your mouths. Just keep quiet. We mustn't wake your mother," he warned them.

Thunder boomed again; lingering rumbles echoed nearer as the storm crept closer.

Dwight's eyes were as wide as the hand-painted bone china plates that adorned the kitchen cabinet tops. He lowered the scuba mask resting on his forehead. A snorkel dangled from wrapped masking tape that secured the tempered glass and silicone skirt to the strap.

"That was. A big. One. It's close. One, two thousand. Five, one thousand. Four thousand. Eight..."

Aaron rolled his eyes. "You're pathetic."

"It. Might. Kill us."

Dwight bit down on his lip and exaggerated the shivering of his body. His eyebrows jumped, seeking refuge under his jagged brown bangs. He clapped his hands over his ears, as if anticipating the next *boom*.

The room dimmed from the cloud blanket that hovered over the house amidst their laughter and clandestine kitchen antics. Symbiotic shadow forms melted into one, painting the walls with gloom, a menacing stain that spread and lengthened to the floor.

A sustained flare of light ripped through the late afternoon darkness. It scattered the conjoined silhouettes, sucking them to the ceiling corners. Between flashes, the pitch reclaimed its dwelling in a back-and-forth mêlée. The kitchen went silent save for the clicks of the dog's nails on the floor.

Dwight embraced himself with crossed arms. His head tick-tocked with mounting anxiety. He jammed the snorkel mouth-piece under his lips. Erratic breaths warned of the nearing storm like a coastal fog horn through the air tube.

"Dwight, never you mind Mother Nature. C'mon." *You can do it,* Zayde encouraged him with an inaudible whisper. *You can do anything. There's nothing to fear.*

Dwight cocked his head. Message received. His tight lips released a smile around the blue rubber guard. The mask glass fogged from his hot nasal affirmation.

"Don't miss, Buttwipe Dwight," Aaron taunted him. He had enchanting jade green eyes, genes for a strong future jawline, and the shrewdness of a seasoned street hustler. He was an alpha male like his father, which also made him an asshole most of the time.

Dwight, who was stuck in the awkward years for, well, all of his years, appealed to Aaron with restraint. Unlike most boys.

He swatted at the air, spit out his snorkel, and said with a trailing strand of drool, "I told you. I don't. Like. That name. Please stop." Dwight jutted his hand out like a traffic cop to cement his warning.

Aaron huffed and rolled his eyes before smacking away his brother's hand. "I. Uh. Don't. Uh. Like. My buttwipe name." He constantly mocked Dwight's broken speech pattern. Many would say the eldest boy had been dealt two bad hands from the cards of life. He had several motor skill and developmental disabilities after the brain injury, and because of initial chromosomal abnormalities, all of which his brother admonished him for daily. And when Aaron forgot, his father was quick to prod.

Zayde rocked forward in his chair with a creak and smacked the back of Aaron's head with a light slap. "Don't be so naughty... Ass-vipe, Aaron."

They all laughed, Dwight not as much as the others.

"Zayde." Dwight slid the mask back to his forehead, with his brows bent for the scold, and said, "You shouldn't tease. My brother. Ass is a bad. Word. Don't feel bad, Aaron." Dwight reached over the table, offering a hug to his brother.

Aaron rejected the embrace with dramatic disdain, as if it were the most stench-ridden, maggot-covered piece of garbage in a hot, rancid dumpster.

"Aaron. Would it hurt you to embrace your brother?" Yitzhak lowered his glasses to make direct eye contact. His tone, firm. "Family can go away in a...snap."

"He can go away. I'd love that. Put him on a train or an airplane and get him away someplace where I'll never see him again. Maybe he could drown in an ocean with his stupid goggles and tube."

Dwight's eyes dropped, as did his fleeting moment of hope for a reassuring hug. "I love you. Aaron. I never want. My baby brother. To go. Away. I'd marry you. Even with your. Angry colors."

"Oh, God." Aaron stuck a finger in his throat and mocked a gag.

Yitzhak rubbed his temples. His face tight with frustration, he strained a smile and diverted the conversation back to fun. He waved his hands like a schoolyard football receiver calling for the throw. "Dwight. Focus. Here. Let's go."

Dwight aimed, closed his eyes, and tossed. The grape sailed through the air, landing spot-on — until it slid to the back of his grandfather's throat.

It stuck.

Yitzhak coughed. And nothing. The old man's lungs were too empty to budge the grape.

He fought to swallow, but spasming muscles squeezed the bulbous grape, drawing it deeper into the blocked airway.

His tongue flicked and hands flapped as he choked. His eyes bulged and then rolled to their watery whites, while his grandsons laughed themselves to tears at the old man's silly, clown-like gyrations.

As Yitzhak Skinner asphyxiated, it occurred to him that, for as many times as he'd survived death, the literal grapes of wrath persisted. About a century ago, Yitzhak was to be executed for being a Gypsy, and once again, because Russians assumed he was a Jew. He'd dodged death again, suffering through both typhoid and sepsis. But those didn't count, as they weren't personal. And again, when he narrowly escaped death on Block No. 28's experimental clinic floor under a similar storm. *That* was most definitely personal.

Aaron's face showed growing alarm. The *nosh narrishkei*t was no longer fun or funny. "Dwight, stop. He's choking. Get Mom."

Dwight, who couldn't always relate perceptions to reality, was fixated on his grandfather's silly movements. He tossed another grape at Zayde's open mouth.

"Mom!" Aaron rose from his chair and gave his grandfather a slap on the back, slamming the chair forward.

Down the hall from the kitchen, the front door opened.

"Boy, it's coming down out there. I'm soaked."

"Dad's home." Aaron banged again on his grandfather's back. "Dad, help!"

"Hang on. Let me get in the door. I'm guessing your mom passed out as usual, while you guys ran wild and trashed this place." David balanced on one foot as he removed a sopping shoe. "Can someone get me a towel? Esther...boys...Dad? *Eizeh balegan,* I can't even put my shoes anywhere in this mess." He struggled with the other loafer and tossed it into the corner pile of shoes, then finger-combed his dripping hair in the entryway mirror. From the reflection, he saw his wife lying under a blanket on the sofa. He muttered, "Big surprise, Esther.?" *Estrie, you life-sucking bitch.* It was the usual routine: unmanaged noise and chaos for David, who returned day after day to what he felt was a cage that stole his life away minute by minute. The faded welcome mat out front was an ironic transom between freedom and confinement.

Aaron screamed again, "It's not working!"

Dwight's laughter and the dog barking were just as loud, adding to the ruckus and confusion coming from the kitchen.

"Give me one damn minute to just take care of myself for a change before I have to deal with everyone else."

Dwight grabbed a fist full of grapes and threw them into the ever-tempting target his grandfather stretched open wider and wider, gasping for the slightest relief of air.

The fruit banked off Zayde's glasses.

One knocked into the lighting sconce.

Another landed in Zayde's gasping mouth.

Dwight cheered.

"Guys, *what* are you doing? I need a towel. Didn't you hear me?" David stood fuming by the door as the water droplets cascaded from his clothes. His tone warranted a response from someone amidst the shouting and barking.

Had Yitzhak fathomed in his wildest imagination his son had the capability of violence in the days to come, he would have panicked more at death's grip.

Instead, at relative peace with the life he'd leave behind, the old man resigned himself to the big sleep and calming darkness, replacing the distant laughter of Dwight, a most kind-spirited boy, who was oblivious to what was happening. Yitzhak had had enough of keeping exhaustive secrets, performing fake smiles, and blocking ghastly memories. It was time for the new generation to live without such burdens.

Hachodesh haze lachem, the calendar is in your hands, Yitzhak offered to God in his adopted faith.

And then a tsunami wave of fear was triggered as he remembered something—someone—in the snapshots of history and horrors flashing from the dying synapses of his brain just as the sounds of his grandsons faded and a cold blanket of death enveloped his soul.

Mortimer.

No.

Yitzhak fought against the clouding confusion in his mind for a way back from fate's agency of supernatural control to *teshuvah*, a return to all things as they were intended to be.

At a time when his spirit should be repenting, instead he clawed forward through the colorless void's walls of regret, toward a living hope.

Light vanished, and fate pulled him into the constricting blackness, wrapping him with paralysis in a chilling nothing that sapped him of all feeling of movement.

How could he have been so irresponsible?

The deal will be broken. He'll come for the bloodline.

In his fading consciousness, he tried to raise a hand and point. Only in his altered state could he visualize the direction of the treacherous house down the road.

Back in the domain of the living, his actual hands remained limp at his sides, unable to show the danger.

Yitzhak Skinner screamed a desperate plea, *Mal'ach*, that God's messenger angels might deliver the warning.

It was too late. *Mortimer will come.*

In the permanent place of the dead, there were no angels, no bright lights or family members waiting in the wings. He died in the blackness of regret and error, tumbling through *Sheol*.

The old man slumped over, falling from his chair when his adult son stepped within eyesight of the kitchen.

"Dad!"

Esther awoke in a deep haze from her Chardonnay nap on the family room sofa. She tried her best to follow David as she reoriented herself to her whereabouts and sobered her wits over the shouting and crying.

Yitzhak hit the floor, jarring a gullet of grapes that rolled from his slackened mouth to David's feet.

"Do something!" David cried as he yanked at his sopped hair. "Esther! Help him, for God's sake! I'm calling nine-one-one."

Sleep vanished all at once, as though it never had been, a holdover from her days at the hospital, when she worked on the

ER floor...before Dwight. Before...it all. Esther dropped to her knees and searched her father-in-law's wrist, then his neck for a pulse. Her eyes welled. She lost her focus and became more distant from her surroundings. Her body slackened in the defeat of past and present failures to revive the dead.

"He's gone." *Just like my sister, Beth*, she didn't say, nor would she dare.

"You're not doing anything!" David shouted.

Esther swept her father-in-law's mouth with a small, trembling finger, probing for more grapes. She then started CPR breaths and compressions. His airway remained blocked.

The old man's gaze was vacant but fixed on Dwight as Esther tried to resuscitate him in vain. Yitzhak's lifeless eyes expired with the lingering horror of a more irrevocable mistake realized in his final death throes. A man would come to the house, by any means, at any cost for one of the boys.

Dwight stopped giggling. "Zayde fell. Down. Is he asleep?" He cocked his head and shrugged. The white snorkel wobbled. "Where did his. Colors go?" It perplexed Dwight. He looked outward into a world unseen by others and glimpsed the dissipating, translucent hue of pastels. He smiled and waved. "Goodbye, Zayde. I love you." He blew a kiss. "I'll see you. Soon."

"Dwight did it." Aaron pointed at the accused. "He killed Zayde. He laughed when he did it. He meant to do it. He wouldn't get Mom."

David stared at the litter of grapes on the ceramic floor tiles being gobbled up by the ratty pup, then stared at his dead father's macabre frozen face. David's expression reformed from confusion and disbelief to tightened contempt. His eyes narrowed as his black brows caved down. He snarled and booted the dog to the wall. It hit with a wet crunch, then dropped in a thump on the floor.

The boys screamed and raced to the lifeless pooch.

David cocked his arm backward in his maniacal advance. In a flash, he judged his drunken wife and the boy she insisted on bringing into the world. Esther and Dwight were both found guilty by a jury of one, while an unknown rage gave birth from the death at his feet.

"You!" he roared and let his arm fly until he could beat no more.

~

M r. Mortimer rocked to the full extension of the mildewed oak runners as he sat beneath the drum chorus of heavy rain and thunder. He relaxed in one of two oversized wooden chairs spaced to fit a glass-covered brass table with a crystal ashtray sitting upon it. His covered porch ran the length of the patio and shielded the elements short of the edges, where water cascaded down from the bloated gutters, pooling on the rain-soaked floorboards.

Above him, a stone chimney glowed muted shades of yellow and orange from the flue opening against the backdrop of the angry gray sky.

The old man drew in a mouthful of cigar smoke and let it roll over his tongue before sipping from his glass of 13-year-old Saint Cloud Kentucky bourbon. His antique rocker creaked with each back-and-forth swing. Under the raging storm's acoustic fanfare, he hummed the Johnny Cash song "Ghost Riders in the Sky," regaling his consciousness about the devil's mighty herd of red-eyed bulls with hooves made of steel.

Mr. Mortimer blew a contemptuous breath of smoke toward the thin white fingers of lightning as the flash retreated from the black. He turned his head toward the Skinners' home.

A mere block away, something had shifted in the world of Yitzhak Skinner, and in the world of Mr. Mortimer, too.

He heard the whispers, not from the same, but another. The whispers were strong. Pure. Mr. Mortimer rotated his head as his eyes rolled back, a human antenna trying to discern clarity through an unfamiliar signal. He sensed the pain and pleading from the one he knew. And yet a curious joy came from the other whisperer. Was it the boy? He could not tell. It no longer mattered once Yitzhak Skinner's silent screaming grew still. A new partnership would soon begin—willing or not.

Mr. Mortimer spat and grinned.

"Akana mukav tut le Devlesa, Soptitorului." *I leave you to God, Whisperer,* Mr. Mortimer said in the tongue of Polish Roma while raising his whiskey glass to the dark sky with respect.

From a plate by his side, he lifted a long bone to his mouth and, with a splintering crunch, bit through the hard outer layer to tongue the rich marrow clot inside.

Chapter Two

Weeks Later
Skokie, Illinois

Time heals the fissures of wounds, unless it comes to a standstill. Then grates like crushed glass tear at the sore, opening it to an infectious spread. This happened to David. His grief went well beyond the *shiva* for his late father, which was cut short to stem the endless Temple mourners from violating their peace and privacy. The simmering day-to-day rage David internalized for so long erupted to a vigorous boil.

He did his best to control it as he shook the mourners' hands. He may have just needed an excuse to expose his deep-seeded rage, which materialized with his father's death. He accepted the well wishes of another man and thought of the newfound freedom he could have with Dad gone. He no longer had to keep a safe distance from the community that surrounded him to protect his family and the true ancestors who were at the root of their secrets. His stone surface softened for a moment. Almost a smile. The prospects of a new life sat well with him.

David nodded to a congregation member. David would say goodbye to the knowledge of his distant family members who remained on the move. Hell, now could be the time to clean up this place and lay down the new law. His law.

And so, physical abuse started in the Skinner home, to accompany the mental battering that had been going on behind closed doors since Esther shared the results of the prenatal screening months before Dwight was born. It was family who differed in opinions that first escalated when David's mother was alive. Now the anchor was cut, as it should have been.

David's eyes wandered to a photo of his mother on a floating shelf. Over a decade ago, his *muter*, Anna, had slapped the dinner table during *the* debate that started with a slip of Esther's tongue when she had a wider and safer audience of in-laws. David tried to stop the uncomfortable dialogue but was silenced by the family matriarch with only her glare.

"The *Sheeino yodel lishol*," Anna said with a forced polite smile that broke to her true stern glower. "The child cannot be neglected. We're survivors. How can we let words like 'burden' even pass our lips?" David's mother asked the table. "Uff," she dismissed with her hands to the lot of them. "*Untermensch*, the soldiers called us in the camps. Inferior. Less than a human. To your father's people, the Roma, they were even less than that. Can you believe such a word exists? Such a word. They called the incurable such names! Even children! Sent to their deaths. Infants were no exception. Rather, the rule. The law." His mother knocked on the tabletop with her knuckles.

David toyed with silverware, impatient. He drained the wine from his cup and reached for the bottle.

Anna pulled it from her son's grasp. "They were Germans and Poles. Their *own* kind. You know what they did to your father and his family, David. They were Christians. And we're going to discuss this vile consideration as we break bread with family — as a family? After all that we survived? As if it were an option? David, how could you think otherwise? You should speak with Rabbi Dratch. Esther," she turned to her daughter-in-law, "you're having the baby. Eat. Let's be done with this. It sickens me to think of it. David, if you were forty, you'd have more wisdom. Until you are, your father and I are here to help."

David scoffed. "Listen to you all. Now you're pious? An...*imbecile* will draw attention. You never wanted attention. *That* is the burden. *That* is the chain we have carried our whole life. This child would require changes. Changes in everything. Changes for her." He pointed to Esther. "This isn't about choice — a *woman's* choice. It's about the choices you all have made for us. Choices that keep us in hiding. Even away from actual Jews who we are supposed to live among as our own people."

Yitzhak Skinner listened to his son try to rationalize a point of view that centered on the word "burden" and how Esther would have to stop her work in the Lurie Children's Hospital labs. The old man wiped his mouth and set his crumpled napkin on the table.

"Anna is right," he said. "Let us never stand before God and decide which of His blessings we, as His own children, choose to keep. We are HIS children, yes? Esther, you are making the right decision for yourself, and the right decision under God's eyes. David, your apartment in the city is too small and too far from us to drive so often." As Esther protested, Yitzhak shook his head. "You'll stay in our home. We will help. Your mother and I can move into the smaller room. We have little need for more space. There will be no *burdens* and no more mention of the word. Esther can help me with my research. I could use someone with her education. It may help your situation later. The community is our family. THAT is enough. Rabbi Dratch adds the window dressing when needed."

Esther swallowed hard, but said nothing.

"Trust me, Esther, your grandfather I have known my whole life. Your father will approve. There will be no more discussions. And there will be no more questions of my faith. This is my faith. I chose it. I changed my name to suit it. This is *our* faith. This was always your mother's faith. You're a Jew if you're a Jew. No one asks to be a Jew who doesn't want to be one. God has both blessed and cursed us." Yitzhak cocked his ear to a whisper no one else heard, then stood and tussled with his left sleeve. "If you will excuse me, I've lost my hunger. I'm going for a walk to see an old friend."

Anna frowned. "Friend indeed. And we speak of God. He's *mullo*. The one who *has* no faith. No God. Your undead Gypsy of the devil who calls, and you follow," she muttered.

"Romani," Yitzhak corrected her as he moved around the table bidding everyone farewell with a kiss on the cheek. "Better to pay a debt with a smile than a frown. The price is the same, but the cost less dear. Dear." When he circled back to Anna, he warned her, "No more talk of Mortimer while I am out. Or ever. It's my business. My burden." He softened his voice and spoke to his wife's ear. "And a secret that must never be divulged, lest he come for David...or David's unborn."

Chapter Three

Present Day
Skokie, Illinois

Since the passing of Zayde, his expedited burial in under 24 hours, and the sitting of shiva, Aaron flicked pennies daily at the locked door of Dwight, who remained banished to his bedroom.

"Come out and play, Buttwipe Dwight! Oh, I forgot — you *can't*. Killer." He flipped the metal door latch back and forth. "I'm letting you ouuuut," he taunted him. "Try it. It's open."

The door knob jostled, but the lock held firm. "You lied."

Aaron rolled on his back, his feet lifted to the wall. "No, I didn't. It's totally open. You're just too stupid to figure it out. Try it again."

Silence.

"Okay, bye. I'm going out to play with all my friends. See you, Buttwipe."

From under the door crack came a small voice. "I told you. I don't. Like. That name. Please stop. I'm talking. To Zayde."

"Liar!" Aaron shouted, suddenly furious. "Don't even say his name! If you were out here, I'd kill you! That's what Dad would do! Just wait until he hears about this! You're nothing but a freak! A killer and a freak!"

"I'm being. Nice. He's scared."

"You're being a turd ball. I can smell it from here. From your buttwipe breath."

"Stop." Dwight defended himself when pushed to limits. But this was a rare occurrence, and his boundaries often seemed limitless for abuse; a trait he received from his mother, whether learned or otherwise. Dwight leaned his back against the door and slid down, cradling his legs in his arms. He said nothing more.

Aaron yawned, growing bored with taunting his brother. He hadn't been sleeping well, although his life had remained virtually unchanged since his grandfather's passing. Not so much for Dwight, who suffered from his father's outbursts and violence.

Dwight, however—at least from the view of Aaron—deserved his lasting punishment. He killed Zayde. Aaron agreed Dwight never should have been born. He further agreed with his dad that Mom was pathetic and couldn't keep her head on straight if it wasn't propped on her bottle. According to Dad, she'd killed her sister, too. Drunken murderer to her core. It didn't matter. All her attention fell to Buttwipe Dwight. It always had. It always would. Unless Dwight was gone. Like Bubbie and Zayde.

"I wish you were dead, Dwight," Aaron said under the door.

Dwight awoke in one of the endless cycles of nights, varying between intense and muffled noises to shrill pleas or crashes coming from below his room. There was nothing for him to do but talk to himself or lay awake and alone in the dark until morning, when Mom unlocked his door once Dad had left the house - lest he receive his own beatings, which occurred often enough.

Zayde? Are you. There? Dad?

Dwight's eyes were of no use. In the dark, alone in Bubbie

and Zayde's old room, Dwight's breathing quickened to panic, at which point he could hear his heart thumping in his ears.

Are you. Talking. To me? Where are. You?

Dwight whirled his head around in the darkness, looking for something. Someone who wasn't there.

Who is this?

A paralyzing wash of uncertainty cascaded over him. The blanket and sheet cover felt heated, and his toes began to sweat. But he wouldn't move. Not even to grab his stuffed elephant for security. Dad threatened him not to move at night. Ever. Not even an inch. However big an inch was. He missed being back in the bunk beds with Aaron. Even when his younger brother told him to shut up at night, it was better than being alone.

The dark was the worst part of being locked away from family an hour after dinner. Worse than being forced to hold his pee all night, every night. It was worse than Mom crying outside his door, pleading with Dad not to go in. It was worse than Dad kicking his dog, Kugel, and throwing away her lifeless body in the trash. It was worse than Bubbie dying in the very bed he now slept in.

There was nothing Dwight could do about the dark in his room, because that was when Dad said the monsters hidden in the closet could grab him. They watched Dwight while his eyes were closed. If Dwight opened his eyes at night, they would be there, leaning over him to take his breath. If Dwight stuck his feet out from under the covers, the monsters could lick, then bite his toes. Under-the-bed monsters would sink their sharp teeth into children's feet and rip them off if they dropped down to the floor. Worst of all, they would wake up and hurt Mom if Dwight *ever* turned on the light switch. Dad said the monsters were angry that Dwight took Bubbie and Zayde's room and bed, and one night they might come to take Dwight away, too...if Dad was lucky.

Why couldn't he have been more like Aaron?

Mom could only say sorry. She never could get help and always told Dwight, "In time, things will get better."

He'd heard Rabbi Dratch call his dad a *shonda*, but Dwight wasn't sure what that meant. He overheard him telling his mom their marriage wasn't a failure; it was just going through a rough patch.

"This, too, shall pass," he remembered the Rabbi saying over his mother's sobs. "Your family will be stronger for it..."

All Dwight knew was that Mom didn't save them. Or couldn't. And if she couldn't, then nothing could. Not even his belief in special powers. Such was life, so how could the whispering voice that seemed to come from just outside his window be worse?

"Zayde?" he breathed.

I can help. You.

"You're not. Zayde."

Dwight blinked his eyes in the darkness. He still saw nobody. Nothing.

"Aaron? Don't. Trick. Me."

I am not. Your brother. I want you to see. Me.

"But. The monsters," Dwight protested. "They will get me. And eat me up. Whole."

I sent. Them away. You can trust. Me. Come close.

"How come. I. Hear you. Like Zayde?"

Come. I will tell you.

Dwight pushed the covers to the end of the bed.

He lowered one foot with trepidation.

Safe.

He willed his other foot to drop to the floor.

Both feet were exposed to the cold emptiness from under the bed.

Slowly, he stood. "I'm scared." He dropped his bottom onto the mattress and snapped his legs back up.

Do you want. Help? Do you. Need. Help?

"Yes," he replied. "So does. Zayde."

He will be fine. He's in. A good. Place. Come.

Soon, curiosity tugged his feet back to the floor.

He waited in anguish. The voice sounded close. But the *feeling* of connectedness to the sound in his head seemed further away.

Come. To the window.

Dwight rose from the bed and slinked past the closet. The doors felt ajar as his shoulder brushed past the opening.

He stretched his arms backward into the darkness to the closet doors to close them—as he always did *before* bed.

Continuing, he groped for the curtains and blackout blind. He gave a cautionary look over his shoulder and back to the closet - not that he could see anything anyway - but he thought it had been closed.

Good boy. Almost. Here.

Dwight felt the smooth window fabric and walked his fingers under the curtain.

He drew the rigid shade back at its end and peeked at the dark street below.

Hello, the voice said near his ear.

Dwight gasped. His eyes widened.

The warmth of pee cascaded down his leg to his ankles and under his arches, on to the cool floor.

Dwight sucked in hard, holding air high in his chest, trying to fill his lungs with mini gasps, but it was as if a large grape was stuck in his throat.

Don't be afraid. I'll help. You.

This time the voice was back beyond the walls and windows.

Just as he exhaled, the bedroom door flung open, and light flashed throughout.

Dwight saw sparkles in his eyes as the room became bright, and his pupils fired to adapt to the gleaming sensory overload.

"Dammit, you stupid..."

"No!" Esther begged from behind.

She was too late.

Young Dwight felt the back of his neck squeeze tight. He was flung backward in the air onto the bed. He saw only the black color around Dad and felt the flurry of slaps and fist blows as Mom screamed somewhere from his side.

"You even pissed your pants." David unbuckled his belt and freed the leather from his pant loops with a swift jerk. He folded it, then cocked back the strap.

The bedroom window shattered with a crash.

Glass showered to the floor.

The abrupt break stopped the beating and wailing.

They froze.

"Did you do that?" David pointed to his wife. Still clutching the dangling belt, he fought conflicted urges to counterstrike or investigate.

"No!" Esther cried. "I swear. David, please. Please, just stop."

"Goddamn, stupid kids!" David jumped to the window, crunching glass underfoot with his slippers. He split the shade off its spool, flinging it to the ground.

David paced back and forth, then crossed the room, shoving Esther out of the way, and leaped down the stairs in a beeline to the front door.

Aaron wiped the sleep from his eyes as he stood in the upstairs hallway just outside his room. "Dad?"

As he exited the house, David called back, "Back to bed, please." His voice was firm but ever calm with Aaron. "See what you've done, Dwight? You've woken the whole house."

Aaron yawned and went back to his room, shutting the door from behind despite the commotion.

Through the swelling of his face and trailing of tears, Dwight stared up at the white ceiling. The layers of peeling paint peeling looked like bleached Pringles potato chips when Mom crunched them on white bread before adding a slice of bologna on top and... *cutting them into four triangles.*

"Triangles. Are better than. Squares," he said in a trancelike calmness. He then whispered, "Do you like. Triangles? Or squares?" After a pause, he said, "Same," and smiled. "You. Scared. Me." Dwight shivered.

Esther paid his words no mind and rubbed her hand across Dwight's forehead, then smothered him with soft kisses. She was careful of the swollen and bruised flesh. Her own tears rolled down his cheek.

"It will get better. I promise. I'm so sorry." She brushed her fallen ebony hair from his face. "Baby, for now, you can't get out of the bed. Never, ever. You know how mad it makes Daddy."

She sobbed until a panic came that stopped her line of despair, raising a new threat to the forefront of her mind.

"Quick. Let's change your clothes. I'll clean this up. We have to do this fast. Go, Dwight. Move. Quick."

Dwight turned to his mom like he had all the time in the world. He basked in her surrounding colors of swirling gold and violet.

"I saw. *Him.*"

"I know, baby. He was furious. He's just still so sad about Bubbie and Zayde. Please. We need to get cleaned up."

"No. Outside."

"You saw someone outside?" She paused and cocked her head. "You saw the person who just threw the rock?"

"He didn't throw. A rock. He used his super. Powers. To talk. To me."

Esther sighed with exhaustion. "I thought...I hoped we were done with the superhero stuff. But I love your imagination. Guess you're doing the best you can, huh?" From the few psychology classes she took in college, she excused it as coping. God knows they all needed their anchor to cope. The supernatural was Dwight's way. Along with his newfound daytime accessory of a diving snorkel and mask, which he wore out of water as if it were a baseball cap.

"Baby, you just saw someone before they threw a rock at our house. It's happening a lot in our area." *Spray painting, too.* "It's just kids." *Hateful little vandals. God help them if Dad catches up to them.*

"No. Listen to. My *words.* I saw. *HIM.*"

"Him, who?" Esther sat up, more interested. Her otherwise pale face was reddening through the aura haze. In contrast, a dull black and yellow bruise was emerging under her eye. "Do you really know who did it?"

"He's. A monster. He has a. Black force field. Sometimes. Blacker. Sometimes. Lighter. Than Dad's. Like a black. Hole." Dwight encircled his arms to demonstrate his thought.

"Black like a black man, or the colors you see around people in your mind?"

"Colors. Not my. Head. It's my. *Super*. Powers."

"Honey, enough with the superpowers. We need to be serious." She lifted Dwight's shirt above his head. "If this thing you can see is blacker than your dad's, you want nothing to do with him. Superpowers or not. It's so dark out, how can you even see black in the dark?"

Dwight gently twisted Esther's head the other way so he could change his pants in privacy. "He's real. And I saw it. Change."

"Change how, baby? What changed?" She turned with a look of deep concern.

"His color. It changed. When he saw me. To red. Bright. Red. So I won't be. Afraid. He's my new. Friend. I felt it. In here." Dwight tapped his chest. "Red. Like Zayde's colors. Zayde sent him. To help us. I know it."

The front door to the house slammed beneath them.

"Shh. Baby, close your eyes. Daddy's back." She tossed his clothes onto the wet spot on the floor. "Pretend you're asleep. Shh."

"No," Dwight whispered. "We don't have to be afraid. Anymore. I can protect you. Now. I have power. From my friend. We're dynamic duo!"

The room turned dark again as the door banged closed, barring light from the hallway. Only a faint glow of the streetlamp down the road entered where the shade once hung.

"You'd damned-well better be afraid. Both of you. You lied!

You *had* to have broken the window! There's no one outside. I ran the street up and down."

David found Esther with a swift crack from the back of his sweaty hand, then tossed her from the side of the bed.

He snatched a handful of Dwight's fresh SpongeBob Square-Pants pajamas.

Dwight raised his chin and squeezed his eyes shut. "Monster!" he called. "I want. My monster." But his mouth never moved.

The bedroom door crashed again. This time down to the floor, splintering the frame and ripping the hinges from their seating.

All whipped their heads toward the sound, but they saw nothing.

Esther scrambled back up the bed, groping for her son, desperate to shield him from more blows. Finding his leg, she yanked him close, cradling him from the unknown presence.

There was a moment of complete silence.

The room entrance was black. All hallway lights were extinguished.

And yet something blacker than the black moved toward them — toward David, who screamed a battle cry of defensive rage. He was tossed like a rag doll against the wall.

"He's here. Mr. Monster," Dwight whispered and nestled closer to his mom.

She tried to cover her firstborn under her trembling body.

A wide, toothy smile grew from ear to ear on Dwight that no one but the shadowy figure could see.

The intruder reached towards Dwight, touching him with a reassuring pat. It then turned for unfinished work as David writhed on the ground.

David begged, "Please, stop. Don't hurt me. What-?"

He was slammed again. His pleas for help were as much about the shocking pain and his inability to comprehend the terrifying reality of what came next after each bludgeoning. In the darkness, he was tossed and pummeled in a brutal, mechanized beating.

The figure back-handed David with another eye-watering blow to the face. His jaw cracked.

The shock wave sent his head back and forth.

Another strike caved David's ribs. He gasped for breath that barely came.

A kick flung him into the dresser draws before he crumpled to the floor, choking and wheezing.

And just as an abrupt quiet appeared to signal the end of David's beating, the screaming started anew to further break the man and his wretched spirit Yitzhak never would have sanctioned.

Dwight fought against his mother's hold and raised his head to capture the curious colors even in the absence of light. He could see a flurry of black moving up and down in the room, accompanied by grunts and crashes as Dad's colors changed from dark to light.

A whip of warm wetness lashed and splattered Dwight's face in a painless surprise. When it dripped to his lips, he lapped at the liquid. It was the same taste from when Aaron punched him in the mouth a few days ago. Dwight remembered that pain, how sharp it was against his lip and nose, and how it made his face feel all tingly. Dad was feeling that. Tears came to Dwight's eyes in the recollection of hurt feelings and sharp pain, and he whimpered in heartfelt anguish just over his breath.

"You're hurting. My Dad. Please. Stop."

The black mass stopped.

Mr. Mortimer stepped into the hallway, unseen in the darkness. *It had to be done, my old friend*, he whispered.

The walking silhouette scanned the other open bedroom of the Skinner home. He peeked quietly behind Aaron's door before heading back toward the stairs. He was orienting himself. Searching for something he hadn't seen for 75 years but knew the house possessed. That was part of the deal forged as he and the rest of the prisoners fled and walked for weeks on foot across the forests and countryside of Poland, while the Russians took their turn at exterminating the Romani people who'd survived the death camps. That was the deal he made so many years ago with a young boy he saved from death. Yitzhak had the books. Mortimer, the power. He kept the power through Yitzhak, who had protection from Mortimer. Saul, as was his nature, just pulled the strings and had the power of a nation.

Where did you leave it, old friend? Where would you hide it from me?

David lay bleeding, broken, and helpless.

He was alive, to serve as a warning of another visit to come. He moaned in a weak childlike voice, not knowing if his attacker still loomed above, readying for another round,

"Who...are you?"

Chapter Four

January 12, 1945
Oswiecim, Poland

I t was a raging storm on many fronts, with no foreseeable calm. Already days late from receiving the news, they feared futile efforts to find and save their man, lest their own necks. They were German war criminals facing orders for arrest or termination by the Allies and Russians, who would hunt them down. Their man from *Die Spinne* (The Spider), who was to be tasked with the future escape, aid, and subversion to steal away SS, SA, Gestapo, and other personnel, had been captured—by their own men.

There was little in their control to fix the so-called "incident." A most uncomfortable position for men who used to be in power and now had none. Years in the making, mission failure was not an option. Gold and other stolen riches were being sent in all directions from the region, to reinvigorate the Führer's war efforts or create a successor plan—the Fourth Reich.

Adding to their peril was one of those unseasonable winters Bavarians in the recovered territories would regale in for years, but not for as long as their unthinkable atrocities would be etched as industrialized murder. History was in the making, and forces were at work to change how evil was defined and men and women would define themselves for generations to come.

These were the plaguing thoughts of the Butcher of Lyon, Nikolaus "Klaus" Barbie, as his driver raced to salvage the operation, while Klaus smoked fitfully in the back seat.

"He was the only man to know where the routes splintered," Barbie mumbled to himself and the guard sharing his back seat. "I saw to it personally. Selected him myself. No one would dare betray such a man." He sucked hard, blazing the tobacco to a bright orange and yellow glow, then slammed it against the back of the driver's seat. It sparked and dropped to the floor. "Nobody who knew what he was capable of. Not one man. Not even that lunatic Mengele."

"*Todesengel*," the driver whispered to himself of the Angel of Death.

Arctic gusts mixed with a passing jet stream downpour ravaged the valley with heavy sleet and hail, while the 6-wheeled wagon fought for traction on the treacherous motorway. The all-terrain military sedan's tires clawed through pools of frozen slush, catching grip between black ice patches to keep from cascading down into the shadowy abyss of the Sola River hundreds of feet below. Official party markings were bolted to the vehicle to avoid unnecessary delays, but the storm, perhaps the wrath of God, fought against their progress with ferocious icy blasts.

The scant light was scattered amidst hailing pinballs and oppressive darkness. The gloomy lighting silhouetted a hazy glow over swaying vehicles ahead.

A bolt of lightning exploded, followed by the crash of thunder. The raging winter tempest shook the car and men to their core. All assumed Allied forces had started a barrage of artillery shelling. The intermittent bright strobe flashes dissipated in the storm, making visibility even worse as eyes dilated from the white bursts and ensuing darkness.

"How did they find him?" The German intelligence officer,

Barbie, restarted mentally mapping the double cross yet again. "Who had access?"

The driver's fingers ached from a death grip on the wheel as he navigated the treacherous route, doubling the speed of any rational man under both the weather and duress. It had been two hours of pushing the envelope in the dangerous conditions.

"*SCHNELLER*," Barbie commanded from the rear passenger seat. "I order you to go faster!" With another cigarette lit, he blew smoke as he spoke. The gray haze inside the car still hung heavy. Nordland zigaretten butts floated in pools of floorboard water, as if they were conducting maritime maneuvers.

The motor pool VIP driver, a low-ranking but well-connected lieutenant, pondered a response that wouldn't end with him in front of a firing squad. As he waited, another wave of freezing rain rattled across the G-4 all-terrain Mercedes like a bucket of nails spilled across a tight snare drum.

"Answer me. Why have you not passed them?"

"Sir, respectfully, I understand my orders, but any faster, and we risk our deaths. We are moments away from the camp." The driver maneuvered another unforeseen turn, fishtailing the speeding vehicle for a moment before speeding up and reining the car back under control. "Steady yourself; we're approaching another turn."

"If we don't arrive in time, I promise our death. Faster!" He pounded on the driver's seat, willing the heavy iron vehicle to reach the destination sooner.

"*ACH NEIN.*" The driver swerved left, then pulled hard right to counter and regain control. He crossed hand over hand on the wheel, then recrossed them back in reverse.

All eyes in the G-4 followed a hulking Opel Blitz utility vehicle drive off and over the roadside, sailing into the blackness below like a three-ton chariot in silent flight.

"*WAS WAR DAS?*"

"Transport, sir. It's...gone. We should..."

"I know what...never mind. Pass the next one or send them into the ravine."

"Sir?"

"It's an order! Send them over the edge if they won't move!"

The Mercedes sped up for a moment before losing control, and centrifugal force pulled the occupants closer toward the roadside edge. Again, the driver corrected the movement and caught just enough surface to right his control, jerking the passengers to the opposite side.

Barbie pounded on the car seat like it was an overworked stallion.

The windshield was covered in a persistent freezing film. Wipers were futile. The driver raised his right arm to mouth level, bit down on the heavy wool overcoat, and chewed it over his hand. He kept a respectful and fearful eye on the void below and ghostly red eyes of dim brake lights ahead.

"Hand on the wheel, you fool!" Klaus Barbie barked.

"I can't see." The driver stretched over the steering wheel with a covered fist and scrubbed at the frost and condensation. "Please, open the rear windows." The pane before him remained clear only for a moment until ice crystals reformed and haze frosted the space again in a thin veil of white. "With the smoke, the rain, and fogging windows, I just can't..."

"You've frozen the glass with your incessant chatter and panting. Dammit, boy. Drive."

The lieutenant turned back, his annoyance at its peak. "You've smoked two packs of cigarettes in the last..."

"*MEIN GOTT!*" Barbie screamed and pointed over the seats.

Chapter Five

January 12, 1945
Oswiecim, Poland

The oncoming vehicle slid out of control into an embankment, launched into the air, then crashed down to its side.

The Mercedes driver veered. He missed the half-ton truck by less than a meter, fishtailed, and slid up to a raised berm just before a great fenced compound.

"*DUMMKOPF!* Are you trying to kill us all?"

Letting out a slow breath, the driver gave the vehicle a little more gas for a final turn. The wheels spun at first, then caught enough frozen ground to move the black transport forward. The driver flickered headlights to guards on post at Konzentrationslager, or KL, Auschwitz, the main concentration camp in the town of the same name.

Iced letters embedded in the metal arch spelled ARBEIT MACHT FREI, or WORK SETS YOU FREE, but they could hardly be discerned in the storm.

The guards let the Mercedes VIP transport pass unobstructed with a flash of lights, waves, and *Heil* salutes.

The three men heaved a sigh of relief with the journey's end in sight. Only Barbie knew the easiest part had just passed.

Klaus Barbie rubbed his hands with the same uncertainty his own victims had before they met their untimely deaths across Europe. As a ruthless intelligence officer, he was used to stress and anguish, but he could be met with a bullet to the head from his own people or swinging rope from the Allies. The future of the Reich rested in Barbie's plan and carefully selected commando enforcer, who had enough history of brutality and adaptivity to ensure the job was done right. Someone, however, had screwed up. Through ignorance or intentions, Barbie remained uncertain. So much was unclear with recent communication breakdowns, greed, and shadowy acts of self-preservation by men who'd already distinguished themselves with immorality.

The car passed the administration building in the campus-like two-story complex. There were no longer incoming prisoners being processed, as Russian forces would soon converge on the town. All evidence was to be eliminated.

Lines of walking dead silhouettes in the distance plodded in a forced march toward the forest.

Bulb lights in the foreground were shrouded under frozen tin saucers, giving off a dim, hellish red glow to guide the way.

The car caught yet another small patch of ice and slid towards the innermost electrified barbed wire surrounding the various barracks buildings. Charged with 3 thousand volts, all in the car kept a leery eye on the closing fence. A soaring guard tower emerged through the sleet as the car slid faster out of control. Catching grip for only a moment, the driver gave the swerving vehicle another power thrust on the treacherous roadway.

As the car spun and skidded, Barbie braced his hands on the seat in front for the last time.

"Herr Leutnant. Get me out of the car!" He flopped back into his seat, took a last deep drag, and exhaled with the smokey breath of a dragon. "I will go on foot from here. We will miss the building in this wheeled ice cavern. I know where it is." He tossed the butt to the sound of a faint sizzle in the water between his feet.

It had been two years since he had been to Auschwitz. The poplar trees adorning the road had long lost their leaves and now lined the haunting camp like vast rows of twisted emaciated hands and broken icicle fingertips. The railway yard was abandoned. Engines and box cars were blanketed with snow and ice. Towering at the end of the roughly 300 hundred-meter opening was yet another glow tipping 3 brick chimney monstrosities. It cast a bright orange beacon that parted the storm and speared the night sky with a perpetual cough of horrific-smelling smoke.

The silent guard sitting to the left of Barbie in the back raised a hand in protest and spoke for the first time. His voice was low. He spoke in crisp, deliberate words. "*Nein*, we will go together." The guard pushed his heavy coat behind a large hip holster.

Even in the darkness of the car, the spymaster knew he was being glared at. Barbie reached for the door handle in no mood to argue. "Suit yourself. I'm getting out."

The door didn't budge. He rammed it with his shoulder, again and again. "What is this?" Barbie demanded.

The guard slammed an arm across Barbie and kicked open the door.

"How dare you touch me? You're here to protect me." Barbie tempered his anger, knowing this man had gained fame as the daring rescuer of Benito Mussolini. He was one of Hitler's favorites.

"Tomorrow, you will be just another man to me. If you survive," the 6'4" Austrian guard said.

Barbie stepped out. His leather boot dropped through a false floor of snowy mush and hit ice-covered crushed brick and decomposed granite.

The guard grabbed his arm, saving him a fall.

Barbie jerked free and mumbled to himself, "Kommandant Hoess had better be here. I hold Rudolf personally responsible!"

"They will all be here," the guard said. "Hauptsturmführer

Brunner, Eichmann, Hess, Kaltenbrunner...Himmler has ordered it."

"Herr Reichsfuhrer had best be here, too. They were ordered not to touch my man! He was to remain in their medical care solely to become emaciated to better blend with other prisoners, only after my orders. That was all!"

"He murdered their guards."

"To save himself and the mission. How were any of us to know what they were doing here? Clauberg, Oberhauser, Hoven, Brack. All of them. Monsters! Experiments. Fanaticism. I hold Mengele especially responsible. And intend to tell him so. I should pull the trigger myself! These special medical branch men are not Waffen. They are maniacs!"

The men hurried past Block 10 across the footpath, giving a compulsory *"Heil Hitler"* to the guard at the hospital entrance, who greeted them with an *"Achtung!"* upon seeing the intelligence officer and elite markings of his guard's heavy wool coat.

Rifle rapport cracked in startling succession behind them.

The battle-hardened men winced, nonetheless.

A series of a dozen shots. It paused and repeated.

Dogs barked. Whether it was before or after the noise didn't matter.

The hospital guard grinned. "Don't worry, they're not here yet."

"Who exactly?"

"Russians. Americans. British. Take your pick. Orders are to clean up the camp. We're starting with the Gypsy camp." He chuckled. "Only way to clean it up."

"We've been called by High Command," Barbie said once recomposed. "Herr Doctor is expecting us. This is my guard, Otto Skorzeny. Group Four. Foreign Intelligence. Black Order."

"Yes, sir. They have been waiting for you for quite some time."

Barbie grimaced. "They?"

"Yes, sir. First door. To the right. This guard will escort you to a recovery area behind curtain four."

"Recovery? Why recovery?"

"Herr Barbie, let us see what this is about before you worry yourself further," Otto said. "Your man was Waffen. He would have given the most specialized of treatment and hospitality."

"They were not to know who he was or what he was. Same with our second man. That was the plan. That was always the plan. They had us searching for them at Lublin, Sachsenhausen, Mauthausen, all the other camps to buy themselves time. I tell you, someone has leaked information with plans of their own."

The escort hurried the two men through whitewashed cinder block halls, where a cacophony of smells assaulted them. Bleach, antiseptic, human waste, and palpable angst. The men passed through metal doors with frosted windows and past the bunk bed rows filled with moaning skeletons, their eye sockets sunken, ribs protruding. Towards the back corner, smaller beds were lined with crying children carrying visible genetic disorders. Men in white suits with red strips sewn to their backs and trouser seams did nothing to console the little ones and paid scant attention to the ranking guests. Screams and pleas echoed from distant rooms. Barbie's escorts pushed another door open to doctors and party officials surrounding a metal gurney. Through a small curtain, what looked to be dismembered black and blue limbs were piled on a surgical cart. Large white marbles were pinned to a board behind it.

A short, handsome doctor addressed Barbie with a smile. He directed them into a curtained section of the room where a lone body lay covered from the neck down, the face indiscernible under wraps. Dismembered limbs covered another table like cast-off parts.

Otto "Scarface" Skorzeny discreetly left the group with another man in the shadows, Nazi Schutzstaffel *Obergruppenfuhrer* Hans Kammler, head of special weapons.

The officer gasped when he realized what they were.

"You've created hell on Earth. We'll all hang for this," Barbie said.

"I assure you, Herr Barbie, he is never better." The doctor raised his arm to present the patient as if he were a prized display. The doctor glanced at the cart and wall of human remains. "Oh, I see. Perhaps you were concerned about these? Perfectly acceptable sanctioned experiments to support our commandos in the field."

"My man?" Barbie gasped in disbelief as the patient turned his head towards him. "His eyes. Look at his eyes." Barbie sidled closer. "They are black as coal!" He turned to the doctor in utter dismay. His voice was a mere rasp. "What have you done, Josef? What in God's name have you done here?"

SS officer and physician *Untersturmfuhrer* Josef Mengele beamed with pride. "That's better. No need to be so formal, Klaus."

Barbie stared dumbfounded at his formerly formidable man, who was now withered, with gauze wrappings loosely binding every appendage. "This is beyond Vice-Admiral Heye's request. The D-IX regime--"

"D-IX is child's play."

Chapter Six

January 12, 1945
Oswiecim, Poland

Dr. Mengele removed a long steel needle from the patient's wrist and disconnected the yellowed IV tubes. He neglected to clean or dress the growing bulb of blood from the injection site, which dripped to the floor.

"Your man gave us quite a fight. One day, he went completely mad and attacked our guards. I suspect the dietary restriction and dehydration were the cause."

Barbie couldn't stop staring at his man, who was unable to speak, with his jaws wrapped tightly in bandages over his head and under his chin. "You went forward with it. You experimented on our own kind."

"Time has run out. If our soldiers are to receive the treatment, we had to accelerate the program."

"There were other options in the hospital. You have an unlimited supply of subjects."

Barbie tilted his head and leaned closer to his officer on the gurney to examine the small bleeding wound. It had clotted. A small scab was forming as he observed the rapid phenomenon.

"Herr Hoess and I received orders from Hauptsturmführer Brunner himself. Herr Brandt ordered the guards to eliminate all evidence in the camp, except certain special selections before the Russians arrived. We cannot allow the next generation of sub-humans to continue, regardless of who controls the lands. It would simply be…irresponsible." He dismissed the matter further with a pursing of his lips in distaste. "Even at the cost of your…endeavors."

"What do you know of my operation? I could have you shot for the mere mention of it."

Another man stepped from the corner of the room. Adolf Eichmann had been hidden behind the other men. He wore a high officer's security service markings and uniform. Lean and as movie star handsome as Mengele, he was used to getting his way.

The room saluted.

"Herr Barbie, this is not debatable," said Eichmann. "Herr Doctor and his team fought hard to save your man. Even after he attacked them for beating a boy who had disobeyed. You are responsible for this operation, which has had…shall we say, *complications*. How could they know he was your man when he came to us wearing a political prisoner uniform? To the contrary, I applaud their initiative."

"He looks like…a demon from Hell. How can he conduct his mission?"

"You are a smart man, Herr Barbie. I am sure you will think of something. If he is truly to be inserted into a surviving *Juden* population, you have an inside man to ensure his escape. What I see certainly resembles the others in this ward. He's as disgusting as the lot of them. The doctors tattooed him as a ghetto Gypsy. Appropriate, don't you think?"

Eichmann pulled at the gauze on the arm of the man on the gurney. The blueish green ink started with the letter Z, for Zigunder, followed by a series of numbers.

Barbie shuttered with fury. He was outranked and checked his temper for the moment. "You made him one of *them*. Herr Eichmann, what other measures have been taken that I should be aware of?"

"I have instructed the doctors to keep a full set of documentation to include all tests, enhancements, and correlating research. They shall remain most guarded by Dr. Mengele under my strict orders of protocol, and Dr. Kaschub shall relay various findings to the Wehrmacht for future use."

Mengele nodded to a small stack of brown leather-bound notebooks on a side table. "I assure you it will remain in my safekeeping."

The bandaged man stirred. He moaned and whimpered.

Mengele smoothed his smock. His face wrinkled with agitation. "We left him with the level of attention afforded to his kind. Shortly after learning he was your man, we saved him with all of our science at our disposal to keep him alive. It was an unfortunate misunderstanding."

Barbie began to speak, but Eichmann raised a hand, motioning for the doctor to continue his explanation.

"We have augmented your man's body chemistry by transferring improved cellular interventions that have modified various stem traits," Dr. Mengele shared, with pride. He glanced at a table of human remains. "It was truly exhausting work for me."

"Speak to me plainly."

"His genetics have been augmented."

Barbie fidgeted with his officer cap. "How is this possible?"

"We simply took a virus. IGF-one. And we improved it. Like insulin," Mengele lectured. "We injected various levels into his muscles to activate transposons. We call them jumping genes. It is a positive outcome from DNA remodeling."

Barbie fought the details. "Sounds like you made him into a monster. Is he still a man?"

"Quite so. Our program was designed for enhancement, not replacement. One of these benefits is the ability to recover from his wounds quickly. Previous subjects have exhibited approximately fifteen to thirty percent increase in strength and endurance. The exact amount, we cannot be certain without tests. When damaged, his cells do not die; they repair. They enhance. Even those with genetic mutations. Now, that's something we all could benefit from, yes? A feature we should all be so lucky to benefit from." Mengele stepped to Barbie and put a hand on the frustrated officer's shoulder. "He has been given a remarkable gift. As an elite commando, he will be virtually unstoppable. You should be thanking me."

"'Unstoppable' won't save us if my mission fails."

Eichmann scowled. "*YOUR* mission? Continue, Doctor."

The doctor nodded in appreciation at Eichmann. With the protection of a superior officer present, the doctor sneered at Barbie. "We have also learned much about performance from our testing here and at other camps. We have the capacity to isolate genes within the cell that improve his survivability in conditions that would have many men succumb to the physiological effects. Look at him. He has recovered miraculously while being nearly sixty kilos less than he should be. We are actually draining him of fluids now, to keep his body as you intended."

"How would you know what I intended? There is a traitor in our ranks."

"An unfortunate incident has become your good fortune."

"You only wanted a live subject for your version of a super race."

"My esteemed colleague, we have ample live subjects. He is no superhuman, but the enhancements have elevated him from standard performance levels to a heightened peak ability that will not overwhelm his endurance and recoverability. Bones, nerves, muscles; they now all heal much faster. Truly remarkable. This and the immunization compounds, and it is only a question of for how long without further tests."

"So disappointed to have disrupted your work." Barbie sloughed the doctor's hand from his shoulder.

"There is not yet in our possession the complete knowledge for blocking entropy, meaning he will certainly meet death at some point. Doctor Reinhardt and I simply need more time and research subjects to isolate the klotho gene."

"So, this monstrosity you've created isn't quite a god."

Mengele smiled as if flattered. "He will age and die, but he will remain agile and strong until who knows when. He will need future cell therapies, but this can be done from adipose tissue," the doctor shrugged with indifference, "or other individuals who have received the treatments."

"What does that mean?"

"Like us all, the patient must eat to live. Provided he nourishes himself routinely, he must have meat. Human is best. While there is an ample supply of bodies for consumption, he would do well to eat tissue. Of course, animal protein can be substituted for relative sustainability. He has to maintain his altered abdominal acids to allow foreign DNA fragments to be digested. As you are aware, in times of war, food scarcity is an issue. We have considered this in his favor. Where there are bodies, there is food. And those like him can serve as a stem cell blood bank, so to speak. The closer to his genetic line, the better. Closer to those augmented, better still."

Barbie wiped his clammy brow. "God, how could you kill him?"

Mengele shrugged his shoulder, delivering a sinister smile. "Cut off his head? Even I can't make a human regrow a head." Mengele laughed, then looked to his peers for their supporting giggles.

"He's an abomination."

Josef Mengele winced. "May I remind you that our patient is fully aware of his surroundings at this time, including our conversation. This, Herr Barbie, was admittedly an unfortunate aspect of our enhancement. Our research has shown us that we could inject a chemical to bring the iris to its original infantile stage of blue. Your man had, as you know, green eyes, so the cosmetic improvement should have taken well. Alas, as we have been working with a lesser species—the Pole, Jew, and Gypsy—you see this negative effect before you. His pupils enlarged greatly, and the iris adopted the black. This may be temporary. It has yet to be determined. We have undergone a series of tests from our heterochromia iris tests on Sinti and Roma prisoners, and as you see by the surrounding light, it does not impair daylight vision, but during the night, your man will be able to see like a jungle cat."

"The intent was for him to *blend* with others," Barbie muttered in near defeat. "I'm left with this...this black-eyed *cannibal*."

The doctor glared. "You really should have informed me."

"Enough!"

Barbie had to work with this outcome, however undesirable it was. But now, these men now *knew* who his man was. This was not acceptable. His orders came from higher than Eichmann. His man reported through Barbie, directly up to Heinrich Himmler as a special division counterintelligence enforcer. He would have to eliminate these men to ensure the secret was kept. It was impossible to do at this time.

"My sincere apologies, Herr Barbie. This situation, as you can see, is quite stable and is shrouded in all your secrecy."

"And what of the side effects? What abomination shall be created if he has future children?"

All eyes moved to Eichmann.

Eichmann shuffled his feet and moved his arms behind his back as he regarded the floor. "Herr Barbie, we thought it best to sterilize him, given the change in cells. He is now an unsuitable reproductive subject and has been castrated so he may focus on his tasks for the Fatherland against the Bolsheviks. We have removed...shall we say, distractions."

The doctors and officers in the room remained solemn and avoided eye contact. Barbie sensed more was unsaid.

His man on the gurney closed his eyes tight, twitched his fingers, and clenched his loosely wrapped fists.

Barbie watched veins rising to bulbous proportions between the white gauze. For a moment, he thought he could see the man's heartbeat. The bandaged man's deep, dark eyes widened to the point where thin, fleshy lids appeared as though they may rip from the black orbs squeezing from their sockets.

Barbie felt the hairs on his neck stand under his black skull-adorned collar. Beads of cold sweat slalomed down his back. His stomach pitted with fear. In the two spheres of black before him, he could see his own imminent death.

The others looked to one another and shuffled backward. They saw what the bandaged man had done in unbridled rage before Mengele had perfected the treatments. They knew he would be near impossible to stop.

Barbie heard muffled snaps as Black Order guards unfastened their pistol holsters. He reached for his own, not knowing where exactly the most dangerous threat would come from.

Mengele's monster opened his eyes in an instant. Scanning the room incessantly, his black eyes gave nothing away from his direct gaze. He was lying to save his own life. He knew Barbie's true man had been buried the day before and neither he nor the raging Nazi officer had more than minutes to live. For the monster, all that needed to be known was recorded in the books. He was now expendable, having proved their concept. The next phases in the human trials could begin wherever they re-established themselves. Unless he could change that.

Chapter Seven

January 12, 1945
Oswiecim, Poland

His eyes darting everywhere and voice quaking from the limits of keeping himself together, Barbie asked, "Can my man be released now?"

Mengele relished his comrade's continued discomfort. "It appears you've agitated him. We're friends here, as you can see. And no need to refer to him as 'your man.' You should just call him by name. Gunthar Hibsch. Correct?" Mengele asked. He still looked like a cat who'd devoured a family of canaries and was obviously relishing every moment of this power contest.

"How do you now know his name?" Barbie asked, confronted with yet another unpleasant surprise.

"We have our ways of discovering secrets as well, Herr Barbie. You are not the only man in this room with privileged access to the commandant. We know that Herr Hibsch is your henchman. We know of his exploits as secret police." Mengele tapped a file stuffed full of wrinkle-edged papers. "We have the contact list, the routes. Everything."

"Gunthar Hibsch is dead," Barbie said.

The men in the room tensed.

Barbie continued. "If you are to refer to him, refer to him as Herr...Mortimer. The dead." He stopped at their palpable relief, which he misinterpreted for acceptance. "If it is leadership's will for you to know, they have surely warned you of the importance of secrecy."

An explosion sounded in the distance. Air raid sirens revved their high-pitched warning sequence.

"They are near," a guard announced to the room. "We have orders to destroy the camp—now."

Mengele beamed with excitement. "Yes. Perhaps we show Herr Barbie our final test."

Eichmann nodded in approval. He glanced at his watch as another explosion sounded off.

Closer.

"Make it quick, Herr Mengele," Eichmann said. "My car will be waiting."

"Yes, sir. Franz, get the Polish Sonderkommando who wears the glasses. Have him bring one of the boys to us from the blood room. Better still, the one who we've transfused to Herr Mortimer."

"Yes, sir. Right away, sir."

"Herr Mengele, I have no time for this. Unstrap my man and leave me with him."

"We need to show you something first. I am afraid you may have selected a man with control issues and one who is not *committed*. His loyalty might be called into question, yes? We must have proof before I can release him. It is my duty as his physician, and as an officer. If he does not respond well, I'm afraid we cannot release him."

"It is not your place to question my staff. I am here to question *your* loyalty! Your...*motives*."

The guard returned with a frail young man in striped prisoner's clothes who led an even younger boy by the hand. The man wore a golden star sewn to his shirt but had other markings stitched onto the fabric. It read, "Kapo."

"Herr Barbie, unstrap one of your man's wrists and hand him a scalpel."

"What is this madness?"

Eichmann boomed, "The scalpel, Herr Barbie! Give it to him, now!"

Barbie did as he was instructed. He looked down at whom he thought was the counterintelligence officer Gunthar Hibsch, whose black eyes remained wide. Barbie could tell the man's eyes were darting around the room through the twitching of his lids.

Mengele dropped a small cloth over Hibsch's hand that held the razor-sharp knife. He commanded the Pole, "Bring the boy closer."

As ordered, the special detachment prisoner, Saul Majewski, referred to by his number, responsible for disposing of bodies and informing the guards of any prisoner threats, brought the boy close to the gurney. Saul's chin quivered. He kept his head low and eyes lower. As much as he was holding the boy still, he was embracing him with the little protection he could offer.

"Don't be afraid, Izaak."

"Hold the boy's arms! Press him to the bed," ordered Mengele. He turned to the test subject. "Herr Hibsch, I order you to neutralize this boy. You should hate him. His blood cells have poisoned your blood. It's made you who you are — a monstrosity of mankind. The most impure of those impure vermin."

The Hibsch imposter slid his hand from the cloth covering, his hand tight around the surgical steel.

The young boy trembled as the blade drew closer. Tears rolled down Saul's cheeks as he clutched the boy's black, blue, and yellowed arms. He had no choice and tightened his grip as the child struggled to free himself and pulled back against Saul to escape the knife.

"No," the bandaged man said, muffled. He dropped his hand back onto the gurney.

"What does this prove, Mengele?" Barbie questioned. "You proved that it is you who is mad. You showed me my man has sense, and not demonic barbarism."

"I am showing you he is not committed. In your arrogance, you have failed the mission. Our unit will continue your mission."

Mengele walked over to the SS Totenkopfverbände unit camp guard who stood at attention in the back of the small curtained area and handed him the scalpel. "Finish the job."

Barbie shouted, "Stop this at once!"

"Never mind the boy. Watch your Mortimer!" Mengele said as he kept his eyes trained on his creation as the Death's-Head guard took the knife and purposefully walked to the boy with no emotion to execute his order. "I should mention at this time that our tests on your man also indicate that he is not as pure as you suspect. Kill the boy."

Before Barbie could respond to the second-most shocking news of the evening, the guard wrapped a hand around the boy's head and thrust the other toward the boy's throat.

The guard shrieked and looked down at his hand to find the scalpel protruding from the other side. As quickly as the guard saw the blade, it was gone, and a force snapped his neck back as the imposter's hand drove the scalpel into the guard's throat with unprecedented speed and force. The guard fell to the ground, writhing in his own blood, gasping for air.

Still restrained by one arm, the imposter grabbed a surgical tray and hurled it like a discus at the Polish prisoner holding the young boy. The tray hit its mark hard enough to slice skin above the eye. Saul released his grip on the child.

The imposter grabbed the boy and drew him close, covering the youth's head and eyes at his side.

"You see?!" Mengele smiled like a proud father as the guard kicked in convulsions on the blood-stained floor. "Your soldier can't follow orders. He is a liability!"

Karl Brandt, head of the euthanasia program, drew his pistol and shot the boy, who dropped like a stone from the imposter's grasp.

Herr Mortimer snapped a restraint and dropped to the ground, cradling Izaak and twisting the blood-soaked clothes into the wound to stop the bleeding.

Brandt aimed his Luger at Mortimer.

An artillery explosion knocked the men from their positions. The officers scrambled to their feet, while the guards went for their weapons. Mengele fled in the commotion.

The power failed, covering everything in blackness.

Another shell whistled overhead before it found its mark.

Russians. The Red Army had arrived near the camp.

Herr Mortimer stood, the boy still in his arms. He blinked, welcoming the soothing sanctuary of the darkness.

As Barbie groped his way toward the exit, the German doctors and orderlies in the wing fumbled to escape. Blood-chilling cries of agony and panic filled the darkness as, one by one, they were snuffed by their creation. Herr Mortimer tested his abilities first, using his own hands. Where opportunity arose, he grabbed any and all metal objects to use as weapons. He eviscerated the men's cores and crushed their skulls with scales, hammers, and chisels.

Another bright flash from the artillery barrage lit the way forward for Barbie. He looked over his shoulder. The horror show of broken, dismembered, and disemboweled men were visible in his wake. Their bodies lay like fallen animals on a slaughterhouse floor. One figure remained in the center of the massacre, his feet sloshing in what could have been gallons of barn red paint. The imposter was unscathed and still protecting the young boy in his arms while battling the soldiers with every bludgeon or sharp object within grasp.

Darkness stole the light again, and Barbie tripped, but he didn't stop moving away from the carnage.

Deep, muffled thuds of blunt force impacts drummed in the background, while Barbie scampered out of the prison hospital. Metal crashes battled with the sounds of gurgles and coughs from men who sounded like they were drowning at sea, while a predatory shark devoured their flailing bodies. Abrupt cracks like brooms snapping intermixed in the blacked-out melee of cold aggression as the one-man horde from Hell advanced upon them with a fury of anger and betrayal.

"Stay where you are, Saul, don't touch the books or the files," the man warned as he scoured the room for blood plasma and enough equipment for a field transfusion to save the boy. The only blood source would be his own. He asked himself, *Will it change the boy?*

Saul turned in astonishment at the man's ability to whisper to the mind, *"Soptitorului."* He added, also in Romani, *"Like the boy."* But he, too, never uttered a word aloud.

You're no Jew, Kapo, the monster whispered back.

To any man who asks, I am. Better to be a Jew than a Gypsy, anywhere. Even in a death camp. I'll take being a traitor over more tests.

The voices exchanged came from their verbalized thoughts. Such was the way of this group of nomads who hailed generations ago from the ancient warrior class in India's Punjab, and whose tongues found roots in Sanskrit and the gifts bestowed according to legend by the goddess Kali. A gift their oppressors knew nothing of. One of the many gifts bestowed upon the monster even before he was transformed, unlike the others, less pure.

Chapter Eight

Present Day
Skokie, IL

In front of the Skinner home, Officer Jose Rodriguez and Detective Stacie Jefferson, of the Skokie Police Investigative Division, killed the mid-morning time standing on the sidewalk, while Moshe Dratch finished an enduring call from his car, a rubber banded CLERGY placard faced out from the visor obscuring his face.

"When I asked who your rabbi was in the station, I didn't think you'd really bring one," said the officer, with a chuckle. "Is Moshe taking over the investigation?"

Detective Jefferson gave the Beat 315 officer a sideways glance. "Chief wanted him to be there when we met the wife. Rabbi Dratch was at the hospital last night when the victim was transported over. I've been waiting on him for an hour. I don't know what he's doing in that car." Jefferson did a little shuffle dance. "Finished my coffee; now I gotta pee something awful. I thought he'd be shorter and have a beard with one of those little hats."

Rodriguez cringed. "Wow. Prejudiced much? I never heard of him coming to talk to a vic."

"I'm not prejudiced. I just thought he'd look like those little rabbis in the pictures. Look at me, do I look like I'd be prejudiced?" she said, with a smile.

Rodriguez raised his eyebrows. "Look, I know you mean well, but even a person of color needs to watch out in these neighborhoods, and even with the guys on the force. It's been predominantly Jewish, but with various degrees of conservatism and cultures, depending on the block. A lot of mixed areas, too, over the past few years. This older area keeps to themselves, but a few younger families have moved in. It's weird. The kids go out and play, but the families don't interact."

"How do they like a Hispanic cop knocking on doors?"

He shrugged. "I grew up here. But they also don't say they thought I'd be wearing a sombrero when I show up. No one says anything or sees anything, which doesn't matter since not much goes on here. You know...except the occasional vandalism or break-ins from outsiders."

"That's helpful. And you've made your point. Thanks." She continued. "Anyway, Rabbi Dratch knew the guy in the hospital. Or knew his father at least, according to the chief. Close family friend." Jefferson checked an incoming mobile text. "Guy kept mumbling something about some Jewish boogie man. Probably a religious thing or something he thinks we can't figure out. I'm guessing B-and-E gone bad."

"No guessing needed," said Rodriguez. "Wait till you see the inside of the place. Looks like a train derailed in the bedroom." He paused. "Hey...you listening?"

"Sorry. Hold on. Just give me a minute," she said, distracted. The detective dialed a number and turned away. "What do you mean he's *out* of applesauce? I gave you four apple squeezes this morning for *both* of them. It's not even ten o'clock yet!" She turned back around to her colleague and raised a finger.

"Look, Momma. You're the adult. Just tell 'em no! You told me no when I was a kid. You still do, so I know you didn't forget. I promise you, I'm not going to pick them up 'til tomorrow if you let them eat sugar all day and drink soda. Do you know how late Curtis stayed up last night? Twelve o'clock. He was bouncing off the walls after you dropped him off. That boy's a monster on his own. No need to fill him with sugar."

She waved to Rabbi Dratch and forced a smile as he approached. "Momma. I gotta go. And you better not be giving him more snacks." Jefferson paused again. "I do appreciate you."

Detective Jefferson stuffed the phone deep into her purse and outstretched a hand. "Good morning, Rabbi. Chief said you may show up. Good to see you. I don't believe we've met."

"Hello, Detective," he said. "Don't let me keep you if you have a phone call to attend to." He ignored her outreach.

"Not a problem. I was going to say the same to you," she parried.

"I understand you're new to Skokie." The rabbi nodded with a smile and slight avoidance of eye contact. "Hello, Sergeant." He extended a hand to shake. "Good to see you again."

"I'm sorry," Jefferson redirected. She put her hand out further.

"I'm the one who should apologize, Detective. It's nothing personal. It's my religion. I don't shake women's hands."

"But your religion has you wear that little beanie hat, and you don't have one on."

The rabbi gave her a wink. "It's in my car."

Her hand remained extended.

"A woman who demands respect. I like that." He smiled but never moved his arms. "Forgive me for being late. I don't mean to tie up your day. Maybe you should be at home, where you can better manage your home duties."

If the detective's buttons could be pushed any further, the man had just hammered them into the ground. Dratch continued, while Detective Jefferson assessed the fire raging in her head.

"This is a somewhat personal matter, and I wanted to speak with you first, before I spoke to the family. I've counseled them as a friend for years since they were first married. I actually married them when I practiced. This is a delicate matter. *Culturally* sensitive, you see? I'm sure you understand."

Detective Jefferson lowered her chin and raised her eyebrows. It was the same expression she wore when her husband came home late and claimed to have had only two beers. She could forgive her husband, who spent as many nights away from friends as he did from his family while long haul trucking across the country, but she wasn't having it with this old school man of faith and rudeness. "Maybe you skip the religious crap and just explain why my boss called a man of faith for an uncultured assault and battery? Are you saying it was a hate crime?"

Rabbi Dratch coughed a nervous laugh. "I don't know how to say this, but the husband suggested something out of a tale. Like a fable. We call them *tsjober majse*, a supernatural story."

"You just said you wanted to talk to me first, before you talked to the family. You talked to the husband? I thought he was unconscious? Which is it?"

"I was informed of some comments he made in and out of his lucidity."

Detective Jefferson cocked her jaw to the other side, raising an eyebrow. "A man gets near beaten to death, and he says, 'Call the rabbi, I just saw a ghost,' or some nonsense like that, and you come running like he's serious?"

The rabbi raised a finger. "Precisely. Ghosts, traveling souls of the dead, evil folklore." He shrugged. "Stories of the tormented dead have been told for generations among my people."

"Rabbi," Rodriguez started. "With all due respect, no ghost did that upstairs. There are blood handprints on the ceiling and high on the walls. Casper the Friendly Ghost didn't do that. This guy was bounced off the walls! He really says a spirit beat him up?"

The rabbi shook his head, still sporting an awkward smile. "We call it dybbuk. Like a possession. It can also translate to a man possessed."

Detective Jefferson waved off the notion, like a mosquito had just buzzed at her ear. "I call it a crackhead. Or two. As much as I'd like to chat, I need to pee." She extended her hand again. "Well, nice to meet you, Rabbi Dratch. If you could please limit your involvement inside the house to just family support, that would be *most* helpful."

He smiled.

She crossed her arms. Mumbled. "That's right, you're too good for that."

"I'll take you both in," Rodriguez said, containing his amusement.

Jefferson followed behind. "Still don't understand how a crime scene will tell you the guy's either crazy and seeing ghosts or just got his butt beat by an intruder. I ain't even set foot yet in the house and can tell you it's always the same thing. Bad people doing bad things or good people doing stupid things. Easy math. Wife beater is in the hospital. He picked a fight with the wrong guy, and he got a beatdown. Nothing super, only natural."

The rabbi turned. "You would understand if you knew the old man who lived here. He once told me the tale of a creature made from the blood of Jewish and Gypsy prisoners by the hands of German madmen. He also told me how the beast of the night saved the Jewish community with a kind of vengeful heroism. Coincidence? Maybe. Does the whole family have such beliefs? Likely. But something happened in this family that cannot be explained as natural. I'm here because the chief asked me to indulge them. Please indulge me. Perhaps there is nothing. Perhaps there is something. Who knows? Maybe it isn't cultural. You can go about your day soon."

"Mmm," said Jefferson. She muttered to herself as they walked. "I've got no time for this nonsense. Give me the forensics. Science is my religion. He'll be telling me the Candyman is the reason for all killings in the Chicago housing projects next."

As the three of them stepped up to the front door stoop, a figure jumped out from the landscape bushes. It was a young boy who sported a snorkel and mask. He wore a red cape around his neck.

"Halt. Who goes. There?" Dwight rushed to give the rabbi a hug.

"Jeezus! About made me wet myself," Jefferson said before taking a small notepad from her pocket. "Boy wearing a snorkel and mask out of water? Yeah, this family's not crazy at all."

Dwight rushed to her, with a welcoming embrace. "Colors."

"Well, all right," Jefferson said, opening for a hug. "I'll give you some loving, Aquaman. Aren't you precious...as long as I didn't hear you say 'colored.'" Jefferson returned the tight embrace. "Mercy, that's a lot of loving." She tried to peel Dwight off but realized it was futile. "That's real heart you're giving off, little man. I think you just made my day a whole lot better." She wiped a small tear from her eyelid. "Whoo," she added while fanning the emotions down from her own heart. "You're just sending something electrical right through my whole body."

Chapter Nine

Present Day
Skokie, Illinois

Esther Skinner approached the door and gave her eldest son a tug. "Dwight, enough. Please. Let go." She tugged again. "You gave a nice hello, let's let go now. I'm sorry, he's got-"

Detective Jefferson grinned from ear to ear. "I don't mind. He's so precious. But if you don't mind, I need to use your washroom. I think he pressed up on my coffee button."

Esther just smiled but didn't move.

Detective Jefferson thought the small, frail woman at the entry could pass for a teen wearing an oversized vintage drab sweater dress, but when Esther looked up and their eyes met, the look of aging and fatigue beyond years was evident. This was not a trendy fashion statement. It was less the physical appearance that bothered the detective. Those were eyes of loss and pain. Eyes of hopelessness. The detective had seen eyes like that her whole life, and nothing good ever followed.

Esther's graying roots weren't visible in the low light, but they were apparent under the sky's rays, which shone a few steps into the darkened home. Her eyes were sunken and bloodshot red. The smell of alcohol soured the detective's nose that early in the morning. A drinker, to add to the picture. Which came first to the visible plight was hard to tell.

"Please come in. I'm Esther Skinner. Bathroom is just down that hall to the left." She outstretched her hand to the detective and extended a genuine but small smile. Her wine-stained teeth added to the pitiful sight.

Esther nodded to the rabbi and officer she'd met the night before. "Sorry, I didn't have time to put on makeup."

"I'm not sure why women always feel the need to say that." Detective Jefferson knew the answer. Still, she said it as much with her side eye as her voice to establish solidarity.

Esther lowered her head and seemed to retreat into her shell of a self.

Dwight gradually let go of the detective and breathed her in as she stepped into the home. The boy looked her up and down, but not directly from head to toe as most people do. Dwight looked all around her. Stacie thought at first maybe another child was standing behind her in the room somewhere.

Dwight turned to the rabbi, pulled out the snorkel mouthpiece again, with a long string of saliva, and said, "Same colors. As always. Bla. Brown." He smiled at Rodriguez and reached out to touch him but never actually laid hands on the man. "Still, Blue." Dwight turned to his mom and smiled. "Blue. He's still blue. I like it." He put the snorkel back in his mouth, patted Rodriguez on the arm, and ran off outside.

"Stay in the yard," Esther called out, her voice stronger than her appearance. She turned toward the kitchen. "Aaron, can you please go out and keep an eye on your brother?"

"I'm busy," a voice called from the kitchen.

"Aaron, please. I could really use your help." Her voice had shifted again. Careful, as if heel-toeing over thin glass goblets.

He emerged begrudgingly into the hallway, wearing a scowl.

"You always need me to do something," He eyed the men and lady filling his home.

Detective Jefferson smiled at the boy as she made for the powder room that was just in sight but not nearly close enough. "Hello, young man."

Aaron ignored her greeting and was quick to break eye contact. He jumped right in, drawing attention away from himself. "The buttwipe pulled down your yellow tape from the room and wrapped his stupid head up with it and his arms, like he was a stupid mummy. I put it back up." Aaron brushed past the small entourage and continued on out the door, stomping along the way. "And my brother killed my zayde. You should arrest him and put him in an electric chair till his eyes pop out of his head and his guts burn."

The detective noted the horrible remark but couldn't stop her rush to the toilet. She flipped on the bathroom light and turned to see Esther walking back into the kitchen, where a half-full glass of wine was just in reach on a floating shelf by the door opening.

Got your hands full, don't you, little momma?

Chapter Ten

Once finished in the powder room, Detective Jefferson witnessed a quick exchange of questions from the rabbi to Esther. He departed, with cold, cursory pleasantries to the policeman in a hasty exit from the home. Esther looked shook. If it was possible to bring this woman down further, it just happened.

"Sorry, ma'am, I have to question him quick before he leaves." Detective Jefferson brushed Esther's shoulder with a gentle hand as she hustled down the stairs in pursuit.

"Excuse me," she called. "Excuse me, Rabbi. Hang on."

The rabbi slowed and turned but continued on his path.

"What did I miss?" the detective asked, jogging across the grass. "That was, like, not even two minutes." She took a lung full of air and tried to catch her breath.

"Detective, I'm sorry, but I have to be somewhere."

"Yeah, so do I, so quit fidgeting with that car door, so you and I can have a quick debrief of what just went on in there."

Dratch flipped his keyring around his finger in annoyance. "I'm sure you can take it from here. I've heard great things about your abilities, such as they may be."

"Okay, so excuse me. Because I can tell you're thinking something stupid...and I don't want you to *say* anything stupid."

He avoided her eye contact and squinted at nothing in the trees. "You would do well to control your emotions at a crime scene, but I'm sure you may be qualified...on paper."

"You need to re-focus on what I'm sayin' *to* you, and not what you're thinking *of* me. I'm ready to continue, are you?"

He stopped rattling the keys and backed up against his car.

"Look, maybe we started off bad. We're on the same side here, and I think you know more than you're telling me. I wanna know what's going on here with you and this family. And I want to know that lady is okay and someone's watching out for her."

"She's fine. I told you. I've known them for years."

"That's what you said. Twice now. But that's not what you're *sayin'*. And you were all nice to the boys in the house, asking the lady if she's taking care of them and has enough for them to eat, but you never asked her how she's feeling with her husband all banged up and away. That's what my pastor in Michigan would do. There's obviously some domestic abuse happening here. If you know something about that, you are under legal obligation to tell me. Or at least morally. Am I wrong?"

"So much loss in this family. A lesser man may call them cursed. She'll manage."

"What's to manage? How long has this been going on? And then an accidental death while this is happening? Do we need to have Protective Services involved? Why didn't someone remove them from the house to keep them safe if something more is going on? Aren't you asking yourself the same thing?"

"That is a question for your boss. I'm sure with your qualifications you can get to the bottom of it, unless you'll try to turn it into a serial killer investigation and put yourself in harm's way, again." He paused to let the dig set in. "Yes, word travels. Detective, I really must go."

Stacie's jaw fell. *Oh, so someone's already been talking. Clearly, you and my boss are thick as thieves.* "Well, let's skip that and go with the obvious of what should be in your lane. You didn't notice that bruise on her face she tried to cover up with makeup, even though she said she isn't wearing makeup?" *Or her arm? Why some have gone yellow but others are a day or two fresh?* "Not to mention her breakfast of champions in a twist-top bottle?"

"Detective, this is your case. If you think she was also accosted, you should ask. If you think her coping means are part of the investigation, you'd best check your credentials again."

"There you go with that. What time did you see the husband?"

"Maybe sometime after ten."

"And the husband didn't say anything happened to his wife? Because in the report, she wasn't hurt by the intruder." Her eyes followed a window and door repair truck pulling over to the curb of the house.

"That's a private matter for the family. I won't speculate deeper than that."

"Speculation? He's been hittin' her."

"Now who's speculating, Detective?"

"If you're a counselor, you know domestic violence. That little woman in there, she's afraid of her shadow."

"She just needs bread and salt, if you ask me or her husband. The Holy One, blessed be He who created her for us as a test. Did you have any more questions, Detective?"

"Yeah, I do."

"Please. What is it?" he asked.

"Which one do you think it is?"

"Which one what?"

"I've seen some crazy stuff and know anyone is capable of violence, but I've never seen a Jewish guy beat up another Jewish guy like that, which would rule out a cultural interest of your involvement in the investigation. Maybe a family member or friend of hers who couldn't stand the husband abusing her? You asked the boy what he saw, and that isn't even your job, as a family friend or faith support."

"He gave an answer, didn't he?"

"That little boy said it was a black man, but not a person of color like me. He didn't even act like I was black, the way he kept going on about the colors he saw. Whatever *that* was. Either you're the first person I've ever met who didn't want to go after a black suspect, or it went clear over your head because you asked about his eyes. What black man do you know has blue or yellow eyes? That's confusing to me. I'm not sure what you were asking, which means you must be thinking something else you're not sharing with me."

"Perhaps you might consider in your report a golem creature," he said, as if it was an everyday occurrence.

"Yeah. That's it." She rolled her eyes. "Little ring-stealing guy from the Hobbit. Sure."

"Golem. A creature of the dead. Given life with the blood of others. I'm not being literal. What I speak of is a legend, but there *is* something. *Someone* who is responsible."

"I'm not following. If you know, you need to tell me."

"That's impossible at this time, and believe it if you will, for your own protection."

"Yeah, I can see you have my best interests in mind."

"Detective, I apologize if you find me brash. Even rude. I am here to protect more than a woman. I am here to protect so much more than you can even imagine. This woman has options. The family has made its choice. They wanted the help of a community but never embraced it beyond the protection it offered. I've done more than my duty. Good day, Detective." he slammed the door, as if to evade a pursuer.

"Good day to you, too, Mister Lyin' Man Of God. Where the hell is a Nazi Frankenstein hiding out in Skokie that no one's seen at the grocery store? Make me have to pee again."

Detective Jefferson watched the rabbi drive off. Her fresh start in a new town was already tainted. Chances were, the whole department knew. She touched her neck. Scars don't always show.

Chapter Eleven

One Week Later:
Sunshine Senior Care
Gatlinburg, Tennessee

"Sir, all guests have to go now."

Mr. Mortimer turned to face the nurse. He moved at the slow speed akin to most stroke victims with lost gross motor skills.

The senior care facility reeked of incontinence that flowed like the regular stream of Sunshine's elderly bodies ferried across death's river Styx. Dignity wasn't lost from their memory, save for those who could no longer recall their own names. Instead, it had given way to helplessness as life's cycle transformed the greatest generation into a shriveled shadow of what they once were, now awaiting to place their hard-earned retirement coin in Charon's bony palm under the auspices of convalescence and senior care.

"Oh, I'm sorry, Mr. Winthrop," she said, not knowing the man had given a fake name upon short-term admission. "I didn't recognize you from behind. It's hard getting to know our new respite guests the first couple of days. Are you finding your way around?"

"Yyesss," he slurred, then shuffled his feet toward the small library.

The nurse sniffed the air; her expression signaled she'd caught wind of something foul. Something rancid and rotten.

"Going to find a good book? Do you like to read?"

Mr. Mortimer turned back again. Drool dripped from his drooping jaw. His dead eyes hid behind large cover-up sunglasses. "Caaarrrdsss."

"Cards? Game time isn't until ten tomorrow morning. There won't be anyone playing unless you join the bridge group downstairs."

Mr. Mortimer shook his head. "Mmaaannn. Caaa-naaassssstaaa."

"Oh, you want to play canasta with the man? That's mister Oo-ster-baan. He's the canasta lover. Remember his name now? Mis-ter Ooooo-ster-baan. Room two-one-six. Just down the hall to the left. He's taking a short nap after dinner. He gets a little sleepy after his evening meds, though. I'm sure you two can play in the morning. Can I help you find your room?"

Mr. Mortimer shook his head. "Reeeeaddd."

"Sure, you go ahead. It'll get kinda quiet for the next hour during the shift change. Just go back down to one of the desk stations or main desk downstairs if you need anything. I'll come back up in a while to check on things. And remember. Oooo-ster-baan. Two. One. Six. But he needs his rest, for now. Don't wake him yet."

Mr. Mortimer slowly raised his hand a few inches and restarted his shuffle into the small reading and game room. When the nurse had passed, he pulled a book from the shelf and hobbled back out of the room and down the hall.

Bedpan bitch.

Out of view, he stopped at Room 216.

~

H arrold Oosterbaan was in a euphoric slumber in the modest one-bedroom assisted living apartment. His head rested on a pillow set atop the mocha-colored La-Z-Boy recliner, and his feet were propped up, sporting food-stained slippers. At the same time, Dateline aired a story of long-lost family members who discovered one another on a Caribbean cruise while seated at the same table at random.

With his eyes closed in a dream state of consciousness, he was oblivious when the lights in the room went out. Nor did he hear the click of the door that preempted darkness.

A dark shadow figure hovered over him.

Hot breath fogged Harrold's glasses, a sight only Mr. Mortimer could enjoy, which he did in full. He tapped the old man on the forehead, waking him with a start.

"Who?"

Mr. Mortimer watched the confused face belonging to the man calling himself Oosterbaan and covered the ex-SS commando's mouth. "Interesting name you've selected. Oosterbaan. I recall hearing somewhere he was the mayor of Rotterdam before you shot him dead in the street."

Oosterbaan squirmed. His eyes were wide yet saw nothing in the darkness. "I don't know who this is."

"My list says you were entrusted with diamonds and accounts. I need the whereabouts of your treasures," Mister Mortimer offered in German.

He swallowed. "I don't know what you are talking about." Mr. Mortimer felt the man's pulse quickening.

The older the war criminal, the less time it took. As these old Nazis saw the coming of their own death, their hardness fell away. Most of them hadn't been wolves in their younger years; they had been emboldened sheep. Following orders, believing in what they were surrounded by, and unwilling to challenge an illogical narrative spun to be the most logical recourse imaginable. A solution, and a final solution.

"Perhaps this will jar your memory. My intelligence tells me you have two daughters and seven grandchildren. They live in Franklin. I will let you speak, but if you call out, I will see to it they all burn alive. Do you understand?"

The man struggled to nod. The message and understanding were clear.

Mr. Mortimer slowly lifted his hand.

"*Das uber soldaten.* Is this you?" Oosterbaan accepted. "The stories. I have heard them. I beg of you. Not my children. They're innocent."

"You spawned innocence? None of you are innocent." Mr. Mortimer swung his hand, snatching the man's scrotum with vise-like pressure. "Tell me."

The man gasped. "It's gone. All of it." He writhed in pain even after Mr. Mortimer released him. When his panting stopped, he coughed out, "*Die Spinne*, the Spider, converted it. General Hausser encouraged us to use it for our escape and survival. The war was over. Who are-"

Mr. Mortimer walked his fingers up the aged man's chest to his throat. "The Spiders, you say."

The old man squirmed, still sightless in the dark.

Mr. Mortimer squeezed the old Nazi's neck. "Lies. Where have you hidden it? Give me the location, the key, and the number."

"If the stories are true, your hands, as well as mine, are stained with the blood of hundreds of your own kind. They made you superhuman from the blood of Jews and Gypsies. And now you steal from your own people? You're a traitor."

Mr. Mortimer laughed. "The Jews are my employer. Mossad. The Roma are my people. I am not your people. I am that which you fear. That which you despise." He leaned in slowly, enunciating, "*Mischlinge*. When they made me a test animal, they thought they were creating a weapon for their own device. I've become their undoing." Mr. Mortimer covered the man's mouth and hammered down on Oosterbaan's kneecap. The bones folded with a sickening snap of aged cartilage and ligaments. He held his hand firm for minutes as the old man screamed in muted agony.

"Tell me," Mr. Mortimer said with a calm matter-of-factness, as if he were asking the man to pass the salt and pepper. "What do you know of the Spider's hunt for the books? Do they know who has the missing books?"

"Books? I know of no books."

Mr. Mortimer grabbed the man's collarbone and gave it a snapping twist. Oosterbaan writhed in pain. "You're lying. You were there with Mengele in South America, before you took bioengineering work here in America. He was recreating his research and had dispatched teams for its finding. Teams they made from hateful anti-Semetic militias. The books were of his initial research and the Gypsy camp. Names. Numbers. Data and places of birth. Thousands of people they'd tested on and injected. They continue to hunt for them."

"I swear to you. I have no idea. Please stop."

Mr. Mortimer punched the man's other collarbone. Oosterbaan screamed again into the palm of the monster. He nodded his head, and Mr. Mortimer allowed him to speak.

"There is a doctor. Fischer. Doctor George Fischer. It's really Brunner. Alois Brunner. He was taken from Syria by Mossad. He works for the Americans and Israelis on a joint project. Surely, if you are working for them, you must know."

Mortimer said nothing.

"Find him. He may know. They continue the work of Mengele. In a lab fronted as ancestry research. It's still genetics. They test and sell to the Chinese, Russians, anyone who'll pay. Even Mossad."

"Brunner, you say?" Mr. Mortimer was taken aback by the mere mention of the name. "Impossible. He died in Damascus under Syrian protection." Mr. Mortimer strung together troubling thoughts of the former chief aide to Hitler, who remained at large for so many years until it was discovered he worked for the Assad regime's torture programs, only to die years later - supposedly - still under protection. "He's an asset of Mossad? In America?"

"This is all I know. Don't kill me. I'm just an old man."

"Kill you? You were a dead man when you left your Fatherland. You know more. Give it all to me, or you leave me no choice. In a few moments, I'll have you confessing to killing Jesus himself." Mr. Mortimer covered the war criminal's mouth again to dampen the scream and began the next line of questions and torture.

M r. Mortimer broke only three of Oosterbaan's fingers before concluding a successful interrogation. The validation of Mr. Mortimer's success was evident, finding the key exactly where Oosterbaan said it was, right there in the room's closet, among personal files and trinkets.

"Thank you for sparing us any additional unpleasantries. I apologize for momentarily losing my temper. I'm just following orders. Isn't that what they said in the trials?" He smiled.

Oosterbaan couldn't muster the strength to elevate his head or respond.

"I need one more thing from you, and then I'll make this quick. I could promise you it will be painless...but that would be a lie. How did Bram Stoker write it? A little something to reward my exertions. I've grown hungry." While Mr. Mortimer withdrew a metal syringe to finish off the war criminal, someone knocked on the door and jiggled the locked knob.

"Mr. Oosterbaan. It's Eileen. I just wanted to check on you after your meds. Can you open the door, please?"

Mr. Mortimer whispered, "The nurse. She has a key, correct?"

The old man gave a slight nod.

"Very well. This may hurt after all."

"Okay, I'm coming in, Mr. Oosterbaan. Can you hear me?"

Mr. Mortimer faced the former Black Order commando, put his hands on the man's jaw and cheeks, and gave a quick twist, snapping the old Nazi's neck before jamming the needle into the hip bone to retrieve much-needed stem cell nourishment.

It was taking too much time.

There was a sickening rip, then a loud crunch as the door opened.

Light from the hallway spilled into the room, and Eileen flipped on the light switch. "Oh, my God. Mr. Oosterbaan." She rushed to the broken and bloodied resident whose bent glasses lay askew across the bridge of his dripping nose.

The lights extinguished as the door closed with a metallic *click.*

"Hello?" she called out in the darkness. "Is someone there?"

Eileen strained her eyes to make out the room's deep shadows. She saw nothing. Heard nothing. Her heart rate quickened as she trembled. Her hand fell to Mr. Oosterbaan's arm for security and met the warm, sticky dampness where his hand should have been.

Mr. Mortimer took a deep breath.

Chapter Twelve

Present Day:
Sunshine Senior Care
Gatlinburg, Tennessee

While mayhem raced outside his temporary resident room, Mr. Mortimer dined over the small sink to obtain what little nourishment he could in the bony flesh that dripped from his hands and chin into the red-spattered white porcelain basin. The blood source wasn't perfect, but it would do. A few morsels, so to speak, before dinner to tide hunger pangs.

While the process of sustainment and rejuvenation flowed through his body, repairing cells and their connections, he cleaned up in his chambers. He folded his soiled clothes and placed it all into a bag, then within another bag. Finally, he stuffed the bag into a medium-sized shipping box. He tore four equal pieces of tape and placed the remaining roll into the box as well. Postage already paid, he affixed a label that was with his personal effects, sealed the container, and donned fresh clothes.

There was commotion everywhere in the wing. Nurses, emergency responders, and elderly residents congregated around Mr. Oosterbaan's door.

He'd have to wait another day for the hubbub to subside, perhaps answer a few questions from local authorities.

Mr. Mortimer exited his room and aired a semblance of concern among the crowd. He stepped back to the side as instructed by paramedics, who were in no hurry as they pushed a wheeled gurney down the usual corridor of death. He shuffled down the hall and took the elevator down one floor to the main level.

"Wwwwould you ppp-lease place this in..."

"Place it in our outgoing mail? I sure would be happy to," the front desk attendant said, finishing the conversation for him. She glanced at the address. "Hawaii. Nice."

"Mmmy sssissster. Herrr. Biiirth. Dayyy."

The woman looked as though she was going to ask more, but with the conversation being one-sided and difficult, she just smiled and said goodnight.

Mr. Mortimer turned with a nod and shuffled back toward the elevators. The security camera above still showed a small red indicator light. Unfortunately for the police, it was one of the few working ones in the building. He put on an investigative show of weakness and shuffled his feet one-eighty and raised a hand.

"Mmmmisss. Mmmyyy sssonn can getttt meee tomor-rrrowww. Doesss heeee neeed. To. Commm innn?"

"Winthrop, right?"

He nodded.

"See, aren't I good?" She typed a few key touches into the computer. "Nope. You're all good since you're just one of our short-term guests with no restrictions. You can leave when he gets here. I'll make a note."

Mr. Mortimer smiled and gave her a wave, then blew a kiss.

"Sweet man," she said under her breath. "Goodnight, Mr. Winthrop. And might I suggest remaining in your room up there, while the staff attends to an...accident."

Two police officers strolled in and up to the desk. They weren't in any hurry to clear another dead oldie.

Mr. Mortimer paid them no mind and pressed the elevator button. He regarded himself in the mirror when the doors opened. For a man over one hundred, he didn't feel as old as he looked. Even without cell treatment for nearly a month, he still felt energetic. He was nearly free from the heavy chains of Saul and the Israeli intelligence arm, Mossad. Their enslaving list was now complete. His only master now would be the genetic match, David. Worst case, Dwight or his brother, Aaron.

Chapter Thirteen

Next Day:
Skokie, Illinois

Mr. Mortimer paid in cash and had the multi-state taxi from the convalescent home drop him off at the local grocery store a mile from his house.

Investigators had asked only a few questions at the senior living home. He gave them a few lies, gave blank looks of incomprehension, and let the saliva pour from his mouth. It was a charade he'd perfected over the years, and it never failed. Mostly, they wanted to know about one particular maintenance worker and whether or not Mr. Winthrop had seen anyone that night who looked suspicious. He was gracious enough to share mixed descriptions of everyone in the facility and added presidential names ranging from Nixon to Trump.

He shared that the nurse was the only one he'd seen who'd been walking around in the desolate hallway that terrible night. That is, before he turned in.

Certainly, a man as decrepit and scatterbrained as Winthrop wouldn't be considered a real threat.

After a rest home lunch of overly buttered and undercooked

orange roughie fish filet, with mushy carrots and cold coffee, it was time for Mr. Mortimer to leave the last Nazi on the list as a distant memory.

He tossed a nearly empty duffel bag and spare clothes into the metal donation box outside the store before going in to pick up a few food items for limited nourishment, but most importantly appearances.

With a sense of freedom quickening his step, it was only a few minutes before he left the store, groceries in hand, and he was headed home to have a bourbon and cigar. Now was the time for Mr. Mortimer to start his own life, after 75 years of killing.

$\sim$

Aaron Skinner and his friends hurled bark wood chips at Dwight, who was impervious to their jeers and efforts to hit him with landscape ammunition. He was just happy to be included and out of his room. At least until his attention was diverted to something else.

Dwight sprinted from the bushes to the nearest tree, a wood chip bouncing off his scuba mask, which rested protectively on his forehead. He had his own target in sight. The monster was back. And his color bubble was bright red. Like Zayde.

Safe.

The old elm providing cover was about thirty inches in trunk width, whereas Dwight was about half that wide across his waist. He would have remained hidden as the monster walked by were it not for his blue diving snorkel, exposed bobbing above the jagged saw line.

The monster turned in Dwight's direction just as the young boy mustered enough courage for yet another cautious peek. The monster was a murky red and turning darker. He was looking at Aaron.

"Crumb buckets," Dwight said to himself.

He lowered his scuba mask over his eyes and peeked again.

Monsters couldn't see underwater superheroes. That was a rule. He peeked again. Sure enough, the monster turned his head away from the kids and kept walking, but it was red again.

Dwight looked back at his house. Aaron and the other kids were running to the back yard. They yelled, "Ditch," and were gone from sight. Usually that made Dwight sad, but he didn't care this time. He had his own plans, thought he wasn't to go beyond the neighbor's driveway. He was never to go into the street. That was another rule. A big rule. One of the biggest. Almost as big as never getting out of bed at night. The young boy peeked again.

The monster was getting away.

Dwight slapped at his legs and looked back for any sight of Aaron or the slim chance of Mom. He couldn't see her sitting or sleeping near the big living room window. He looked up to her bedroom window.

No Mom. No Aaron. None of their feelings of colors. He was on his own.

Dwight scanned for the monster's whereabouts and counted in a whisper that was still louder than a conversational voice. "One, three, four, two, seben." He took a deep breath and sprinted. He passed the forbidden driveway. And another. And another. He was now four houses away from home and hiding behind a tree the monster had just passed.

"Whoa. I made it. *Phew*," he said, still in a voice loud enough to wake the dead.

Dwight tried to catch his breath. He hugged the tree, slowly breathing in and out, long and deep, just like his teacher said to do when his thoughts felt overwhelming. That's how superheroes got their power back.

"Thank you. Tree. For saving. Me."

Dwight looked back toward his house but couldn't see it, a large hedgerow blocking the view. Now he was on his own and out of sight.

Dwight was farther than he'd ever been away from home. He whispered subconsciously, *Where are. You?*

Dwight lifted his mask and poked his head around the tree trunk to find the monster.

Gone.

Dwight scanned to his right across the street and down the sidewalk.

No monster.

He craned his head just a bit further.

Nothing.

"Crumb buckets," he stomped. Disappointed, Dwight lowered his mask, opting for a swim back home in case the monster was hiding in wait for him. He'd have to be fast so Mom wouldn't come out looking. Dad was still in the hospital from the "robber" who'd given them all a beating. That was what Mom had told the police. Mom had told him to keep it a secret, so that was what he did. Dwight listened to Mom. He rehearsed what she'd told him in his mind...he kept it. He was good at keeping secrets. Like Mom.

Dwight crouched to remove a rock that was caught in his shoe, digging in just below his ankle. It was then a dirty black shoe appeared from behind the tree trunk.

"Oh, no," he said aloud and ducked back.

Dwight's breathing grew faster. He could feel his heart thumping. "Save me. Mr. Tree." He gulped a hard swallow.

The monster's other shoe came forward.

Big shoes.

Big like Dad's. Dad was still a monster. But he wasn't the baddest monster in the neighborhood, at least not anymore. Besides, he wouldn't be coming home from the hospital for another day.

Without making a move, Dwight visualized his home and how far he was from it. If he ran using all his powers, he could make it in maybe 24 or 97 or 40 steps.

Dwight started counting down, to himself this time. Eleben. Eight. Five. Nine. FOUR!

He spun and launched his first great sprinting stride. He looked up to see the monster towering above him, as tall as the elms themselves.

Dwight whipped his head back to the tree roots. The shoes were still there. Two? He faced the monster. He looked up then down. The monster wore socks, with a big toe sticking out of a hole. He'd tricked him! *Crumbuckets.* Darn monster! At least he wasn't a shape-shifting *shayd* demon, just like Zayde had told him in bedtime stories. And no chicken feet.

Struggling to catch his breath, Dwight lifted his head again to face the beast.

The monster raised his glasses.

In a trance-like state, Dwight shook his head in disbelief. "Not all black. Black eyes. Dark gray. Force. Field. Today. Black. Was Dad's. Colors."

Peekaboo! the monster whispered.

Dwight felt his legs weaken, and his breathing caught high in his chest. There was nowhere to go! The monster would get him! The monster would *eat* him. Dwight turned again in a panic and ran straight into the tree.

The last thing he remembered...was the smell of a dead animal, rotting on the road, before his consciousness vanished in a cyclone of red.

~

Mr. Mortimer lowered the groceries, slid on his shoes, and scooped the child up in his arms.

"We meet again, Dwight."

The boy's coat and shirt bunched up, exposing his bare back.

Mr. Mortimer frowned as he counted the visible gray-yellow bruises. Burning heat coursed through Mr. Mortimer's body.

If Dwight was awake, he would have seen the darkest aura color circling the monster's form yet.

I should have killed your son, Yitzhak. Deal or no deal. Besides, I must eat.

Mr. Mortimer cradled the boy in his arms, squeezing tight, just as he had nearly a century ago with the boy's wounded grandfather. He smiled and let Dwight's warmth of innocence extinguish the scorching fire in his heart.

"Don't worry. We're going to make this all go away, Mister Crumb Buckets." He smiled. "You and I will make a new deal."

Chapter Fourteen

Next day:
Skokie, Illinois

The name was on a sign only miles from his own home. How Mossad had missed this was unsettling, but he understood, given the Reich's ability to gain false papers and create currency with nation states through the exchange of information.

The office was above other commercial storefronts in an older part of town. The faded orange brick of the building made the rectangle complex look like a carved pumpkin, its eyes the white draped windows, old rusty air conditioning units as the pupils. Tattered awnings were the brow, and lower level painted wooden doors the pegged teeth of the Jack-o'-lantern. The sides of the structure were a contrasting pale white. A "For Rent" sign had dipped to the side, its masking tape's stickiness giving out. The place was a perfect gray man. Something one would walk past a million times and not remember a thing. It was uninteresting enough that no one would poke around with curiosity. Perfect for the inhabitant, if the information was correct.

Mr. Mortimer climbed a narrow staircase that went straight up and T-boned to two doors with old round brass knobs. The one to the left had two deadbolts. No name. To the right, only a locking knob. No deadbolts. A sign that read, "Reception."

Mr. Mortimer opened the door to find an older woman sitting behind a small metal desk. She was reading a magazine when he entered the nearly empty room with no décor. A small radio on the desk played classical music.

Without looking up, she said, "Across the hall. Sit down. He'll be with you in a moment. I have to buzz you in and alert him."

As quickly as he'd entered, Mr. Mortimer departed and found himself in the opposite office. Doors all unlocked until he turned and locked them all.

The doctor's chambers were handsome in appointment. The wall paint was a rich forest green. Built-in oak bookcases lined the walls under the stained wood trim crown moldings. The furniture leather. The desk, heavy. Large. Lighting dim.

Mr. Mortimer heard steps approaching on the other side of the door before hearing the turn of the knob and squeak of the door. The door squeaked open on rusted hinges.

He turned to address exactly what he'd expect but hoped he wouldn't see, which meant he'd been betrayed. Before him stood a conservatively dressed man, perhaps in his eighties, probably older. The man's liver spots matched the heavier lines of the brown, black, and green sport coat.

"I appreciate you seeing me on such short notice, Dr. Fischer," Mr. Mortimer said.

The doctor crossed the room and extended a hand. "Mr. Schmidt. It is Schmidt, correct?"

"Yes," Mr. Mortimer confirmed. The man's hand was cold. Bony. Frail. The man's accent was slight.

In kind, Dr. Fischer appeared to size up his new client. "I understand you were referred to me, but my assistant stated you preferred to share in person. Would you mind sharing it with me?"

"Alois Brunner."

"Ah." The doctor turned and found refuge behind his desk. "At long last. Please. Please. Sit. I assumed it was you when you chose not to remove your dark glasses." The doctor leaned back in his chair and drummed his fingers on the mahogany desk. "Seventy-five years you've been hunting your own people. Why? Why would you look to harm the very people who gave you such a gift?"

"The hunt is over. You are a bonus to my keepers." Mr. Mortimer was calm.

"Your last? The last Waffen? Nazi? Fascist? Racist? White supremacist? My friend, I'm afraid it is you who has been the one hunted. How else would you have found me within your own town after all these years? More than coincidence, I should think."

Mr. Mortimer's attention was more than piqued. He was stunned.

The doctor shook his head and chuckled. "What did you expect? A marquis sign that said, 'Third Reich Headquarters?'" Dr. Brunner grinned. The cat had the canary. "Herr Mortimer. While you have been working a century-old list of names, mercilessly murdering high-ranking Nazi officials. How do you think you found men who didn't *want* to be found? Men protected by governments. And yet no one found it important enough to hunt *you* down? You were given the weak ones we fed to Mossad to protect ourselves. Fed from the CIA the assets they no longer valued. The CIA is the very organization that gave us protection, so we would work against the Bolsheviks."

"I found you. I had to torture the man who informed on you."

"You found me because we gave it to you. The Black Order is alive and well. Who do you think helped fund the Jew's lab with war reparation monies? *You* are the last on the list. Someone must be held accountable, and there can be no evidence in the public eye. The Germans want you dead. The Jews can't let you live. The Gypsies...well, they do not know what is in store for them. The great round-up encore. And this time, they have nowhere to run. Nowhere to hide. They are a pariah to all. To all but us. We shall harvest them, yet again."

The sound of footsteps drew closer to the office suite. The doctor raised his phone in a prideful display. "We know where to find the books. We will find the gold that is your people with our serum running through their vermin blood. And we will continue building our armies in the shadows."

Knocking on the door.

Mortimer closed his eyes and whispered the ancient words of suggestion.

The doctor's eyes widened, then blinked. He retrieved a revolver from the desk. Pointed it at the door, then to Mr. Mortimer. "It may not be the serum you received, but it keeps me alive, and you Gypsies out of my head."

As the doctor fired, Mr. Mortimer was upon him. The man had longevity but limited strength. Mr. Mortimer wrapped himself around the man's back and reached across his skull. Mortimer dug his fingers into Dr. Brunner's eye sockets. With a sharp twist, the man's neck snapped.

Kicks assaulted the heavy wood bound to the reinforced frame by the sturdy metal locks.

Mr. Mortimer yanked the doctor's head again.

Gunshots cracked in succession, making short work of the locks. The door bounced open.

Heavy curtains flapped in the breeze of an open window. Alois Brunner's head lay bleeding out on a leather desk pad, his body a broken heap on the floor.

~

A cross town, two men sat behind the soaped-out glass window of an old empty diner in silence, watching buses pass by. They each scanned the sidewalks for someone recognizable. One man looked for a resemblance whose only description had come from a classified dossier; seventy years old. The other man looked for a familiar face. Still, he carefully examined each pedestrian's gait, dress, and posture, just to make sure. Habits die hard. And Mr. Mortimer hadn't died yet.

"Where is your old hunter, Saul?" the younger man asked the former Auschwitz kappo, now Mossad heavy.

"*My* old hunter? You mean Israel's. And do you really want to know where? Or do you want to know *why* we are waiting twenty minutes now for a man who has not shown up? It's really not a *where*, Adam; it is a *when*. Is it not? Language precision is more than good practice; it is a communication courtesy. And where do you have to be that you cannot sit and wait patiently with an old friend and enjoy the silence of the morning and goodness of this day God has granted us?"

"No riddles, no sermon, Saul. I forget you're about as old as this assassin, and as cantankerous. Amazing that neither of you are dead yet."

"You should be more respectful, Adam. I knew your father."

Saul got up from the vinyl 1960s era restaurant chair to regard the chalkboard menu above the grand deli counter. He stuffed his hands deep into his pockets, craned his neck, and squinted to read the colored writing hanging above the refrigerated encasements.

"They used to have excellent food here. Do you know what this year marks?"

Adam replied, "No clue, but I'm sure you're going to tell me."

"Seventy-five years. It's been seventy-five years. The gypsy saved me, and I saved him. I continue saving his life to this day, but he doesn't realize just how much. He has no idea how much we actually know of him. But I knew he had to stay close to the young boy. Well, not young anymore—dead. Poor little Izaak. They were going to kill him then. Shoot him."

A young Semitic-looking girl keeping guard stopped typing text messages on her mobile device and looked up to assist this elderly spy master who clearly needed help. She knew he would have a question. He had a question every day for the past week.

"Sir, can I help you with something today?"

"Well, yes. Yes, I think you can. Rachel. It is Rachel, correct? IDF?"

The young raven-haired girl offered a genuine smile. Her name was indeed Rachel, and she'd validated this every day for the past week as they conducted secretive meetings within Saul's old networks.

"Yes, sir. It is Rachel. You've read it on my military file."

"Oh, yes, yes, beautiful women of the IDF."

Adam continued looking out the window, not bothering to dignify the statement.

"Rachel, have I had the kugel or hash yet this week?"

Rachel smiled again. "You want me to order something for you now?" It was the same routine. "Yes, sir, you have had it every day."

"Fine, Rachel. In that case, I'll have a mish-mosh bagel, lox, and chive schmear. Little egg on the schmear, not too much caper. If they have a thick slice of tomato, throw it on. No onion, unless it's Bermuda. My friend here will have the kugel and hash. If someone could cook, you wouldn't need to go out for it."

Adam, who had been increasingly annoyed by Saul this morning, was now even more distracted by Saul's antics and completely forgot about his late guest as he sought to protest the food order.

"Saul, please, you don't need to order for me. I can handle myself. Rachel, please, no hash and kugel. Just a coffee. I had something at the hotel."

"Rachel, be a good girl and put his order in, as I have suggested. You can leave us now. We're safe."

The young girl reddened. It wasn't a blush. She nodded to another man standing in the back.

"Adam, did you see her blush? Her cheeks, her clavicle? She is a trained killer, paid this morning to watch two men. And she has to take food orders. How fair is that for equality? Pretty woman like that bringing food back into an empty building? That should strike people as odd, don't you think, hmm? These neighborhoods have eyes. They see what they wish to see and don't see what they don't want to see. It has always been so...

"And what they don't see are customers, and what they do see are other businesses that go out of business when there are no customers. So, why does this closed deli have people inside who aren't doing construction or cooking? They do not know. Of course, WE do know. And in reality, they know, too, which makes this location exposed, not hidden...dangerous. Irresponsible. What does this place do but raise too many questions?

"Look there: See the office building there, behind closed doors? There, that makes sense. Like the lab. Like Dr. Brunner. But a restaurant that serves no customers and keeps its doors locked?

"And look at me! I have a granddaughter who lives nearby. Esther. Who is more like me than anyone else in my family. I haven't seen her in years. Why? Because it raises too many questions. Do you hear what I am saying?"

"Then why do you send that girl Rachel out for meals every day this week? Of course I know. You're an ancient misogynistic relic who still maintains methodologies and forgotten operations that are old, dangerous, and irrelevant to today's threats. Hmm. Nazis or Arabs, who should I be concerned with?"

"We all come from Abraham. Please don't interrupt."

Adam waved a hand of surrender to the simple lecture that had quickly jumped from the rumination of the old man to a lesson in spycraft. Indeed, Saul's observations made sense, and the deli was Adam's responsibility. A foreign intelligence safehouse in Chicagoland.

"You've made your point, Saul. It will be fixed."

"Fixed? Adam, I'd never be so presumptuous to let you know what needs to be fixed in your own territory. I'll be gone soon. I know why you are here. What kind of a *mashugana* do you think I am? I am simply trying to explain that the corned beef hash is very good, and I am glad you ordered it. *Mosel Tov*. Even if you want to kill my man, remember, you're an asset. Not an officer. That makes you expendable, too."

The old man approached the younger 40-year-old Mossad Israeli intelligence asset and grasped his hand. He lowered his voice and moved closer to Adam's ear to make a discrete statement.

"Adam?"

"Yes, Saul?"

"Do you want to be trusted?"

"Yes, Saul."

"Do you want autonomy to make your own decisions?"

"Yes, Saul."

"Did you really kill over twenty Hamas bastards when you were in the unit?"

"You know I did, Saul."

"RACHEL! WHERE'S MY FOOD?"

The shout startled Adam, and he nearly tripped on himself, shuffling away as Saul doubled over in laughter. As he guffawed, Saul managed to take the floor yet again.

"Adam. So sorry. Hey, where's our old hunter? He's late. You feel proud of your legendary feats, but do you know that our man killed over twenty men in less than an hour, all while holding a young boy in his arms? In the dark."

"Fables, old man."

"Fables? No...nightmares, I should think. I knew from what I saw or could not see before me was both a righteous angel and a fallen one, at the same moment."

"You are telling me a man of your faith believes there is a hell? An angel of death?"

"I believe what I've seen. And...it's what I have seen that I still cannot believe. I believe you have orders to kill him or turn him over to authorities as a Nazi, now that Efraim Zuroff and the Wiesenthal Center's war crimes investigators have received a report of him. It would be difficult to have a trial, since Israel has benefited from his use. Therefore, it must be the latter. And I believe that since Mossad doesn't have a wet team here in America, you have given all intel to these Nazi thugs to keep our hands clean." Saul ran a finger across his own neck. "I believe it will be a long day." His eyes widened. "Which reminds me, I must be careful of my own thoughts. You never know who's listening. The whispers of a gypsy go far and wide. And Mortimer's Gypsy blood goes to the very beginning. He has abilities we have not yet seen. I believe this will be a very long day."

Chapter Fifteen

Skokie, Illinois

As a public Pace bus edged to a curbside stop, Adam cracked his neck, regarding the large vehicle's window for a moving figure, hoping the hunter had finally arrived.

Adam turned and asked, "Is that him? Did he get off?"

Saul moved closer to the smeared window, trying to get a closer look. "He'll tell me."

Returning to his surveillance, Adam appeared focused on something or someone. "I think it's him, but he's taking forever. What's he looking at? Does he know where this place is? That can't be him. It's a man as old as you. He looks like he's asking for directions and pointing to one of the buildings next door. Now he's talking to some kids."

"Oh, no. Not Mr. Mortimer. The man hates children." Saul turned his head to look at Adam. "The man hates everyone."

"Perfect. Then where is your damned Nakam Nazi?" Adam looked down at his watch again. Nearly an hour late. "The only one passing by is this old fart." Adam turned to Saul, who was now smiling.

"Here we are, Adam. Your Nazi, my Nakam revenge asset for our own reparations. Mr. Mortimer is here. I would suggest you mind your tongue. He has brought much revenge and riches back to Israel."

Adam stared in disbelief. This could not be the man who'd killed hundreds of Nazi war criminals and government-hidden German agents, many of whom met their fates only in the past decade when they were finally discovered. Men who'd been protected from prosecution by Western intelligence agencies to fight in the Cold War shadows. But they couldn't be protected from Mr. Mortimer. No one had been able to stop him.

"Saul, there's no way. This guy can't be less than ninety." Adam gasped as Mr. Mortimer lifted his glasses and peered through the whited-out window. Cold black eyes locked on Adam's. He remained transfixed on Mr. Mortimer as the ultimate killer of men strolled into their presence.

"Careful, Adam. If you gaze too long, he'll steal your breath. I told you, he comes from the gates of Hell itself."

"My God."

"Hardly, Adam. Hardly."

Within moments, Mr. Mortimer and Saul greeted one another with a hearty embrace and a series of kisses.

Adam wore an ashen look of terror.

"It is so good to see you, Mr. Mortimer," said Saul.

"As always, Saul." Mr. Mortimer turned to the stranger but said nothing.

"You had to do it, didn't you, my friend? You had to lift your glasses and make this poor boy piss his pants before I could make a proper introduction."

Adam reached out his hand. "I'll be your new handler. We'll be working together for the next day or so to ensure all financial matters have been settled, and you have transferred all that you've collected."

Mr. Mortimer ignored the hand. He turned his head to Saul.

"I finished the last one. My debt is paid." He reached in his pocket and pulled out a folded paper square. "This is my final collection."

"Let us sit." Saul cast an eye on Adam simply to play along, then opened the paper and swirled the content of cut diamonds with his knotty finger. "How many are there? My eyes can't count. Twenty? Thirty?"

Mr. Mortimer retrieved a stack of packets from another pocket that were rubber-banded together. "Twenty packets. Each with roughly thirty diamonds."

"You brought over six hundred diamonds on a Pace bus?" Adam asked in yet another state of disbelief. "That's got to be over a million dollars. Are you senile, too?"

"Eleven. Over eleven million," Mortimer corrected.

"How do we know that's all? Did you keep any for yourself?" Adam snapped.

"Saul," Mr. Mortimer said. "Put this child in a corner, or I will."

"Adam, please. He's delivered millions to our country--"

"No! I have had it with this spooky old bastard! I need to be sure!" Adam grabbed Mr. Mortimer by the arm and jerked him around.

Saul raised his eyes from the riches. "Adam, you mustn't." He jumped up to stop the inevitable from happening. "Not now. Please. I have to speak with him. Oh, God," he said before clutching at his chest.

Chapter Sixteen

Mr. Mortimer laid Saul on the discolored mosaic tile floor. He pillowed the old man's head in his hand. Rachel returned through the rear with breakfast, which she casually dropped to the floor. She sauntered over to Saul, indifferent about her security duty to a disrespectful man whose usefulness had long passed.

Adam lost it. "You guys need to help him!" Rachel dropped the bundle of foodstuffs onto the table. Adam stared at her. "Rachel, do you have medical training?"

"Field wounds. Not this. And we can't blow our cover by calling an ambulance either."

"Back away." Mr. Mortimer caressed Saul's head with his hand and said nothing. "She's right. You can't call emergency services here. It won't do you any good to take him to a hospital."

"Shouldn't we elevate his feet or something? Is it a heart attack?" Adam looked at the two for answers.

Rachel kept her hands on her hips. "Adam. It's not worth the risk."

Mr. Mortimer nodded. "Agreed. Leave him."

Adam paced around Saul's body, stomping his feet like a fitful child. "Oh, sure, so you can keep everything you've stolen."

Mr. Mortimer ignored the brash Israeli spook. "I felt a blockage by the slowed blood flow in your pulse. Saw it straining in your neck. You would have been a dead man in a week by your own genetics and diet. It's time to sleep, old friend."

"Friend. Neither of us killed each other for our own survival." Saul laughed. "Adam is young, but he'll take care of you."

Mr. Mortimer whispered in the mind's tongue, *You abandoned me after all these years. It's my turn to be the Judas.*

Saul's eyes widened with the epiphany of something pleasant smelling on Mortimer's lips, which was not the norm. He wheezed and moved his own numbed lips, but no words escaped. *Poisoned?* he whispered back. *How fitting. You, too, were dead as soon as you walked in the door.*

Mr. Mortimer smirked. *We'll see.*

Adam stopped his circles. "Wait, we have proper papers. This entire operation is back stopped."

"Tell that to the feds across the street in that van," Mortimer bluffed. "They knew who you were as soon as you came into the country."

Saul fought the effects of the poison. His fingers motioned Mr. Mortimer closer. With everything he had, he forced out, "They funded Yitzhak's lab. Since the beginning. The men you killed appeased both sides. It's over. No one wants to remember our story. The world needs hate. You're dead if you run. Dead if you stay. They will find you and the Roma." Saul swallowed hard. His breathing hiccupped.

"Dirty kapo." Mr. Mortimer shook him to renewed alertness.

Saul beamed and closed his eyes. *They have the cell treatments. They'll never give them to you. You're dying now as we speak unless you choose to eat your own people. The Nazis as we knew them are nearly gone. The hate remains. It spreads.*

Adam leaned in. "What is he saying? What are—" The young intelligence professional paused. His nose scrunched as he sniffed the air. Leaned in closer to Saul's mouth. "Something foul. But bitter. And sweet. Almond." His eyes rose to the stranger. "AC-

Hydrogen cyanide. You poisoned him!" Adam made the mistake of grabbing Mr. Mortimer for a second time.

Discovered, Mr. Mortimer grasped Adam's hand, giving it a wrist lock twist. He freed his other hand from Saul and struck Adam's elbow with a wrenching leverage pivot that sent the young man into the table and chairs.

Adam shot a back kick at Mr. Mortimer, but it was caught mid-strike. Mr. Mortimer hammered down on Adam's leg.

He howled in pain. Through it, he reached for a pistol.

Foreseeing the threat, Mr. Mortimer fisted a table setting of silverware. He thrust a bundle of fork, knife, and spoon into Adam's throat with superhuman force. Adam tumbled back, the cutlery handle tips protruding from his neck. Gasping for air and choking on his own blood, he faded fast.

Mr. Mortimer dropped his eyes as he felt the spirit of Saul slip away. "I'll see you in Hell."

Chapter Seventeen

M r. Mortimer turned to exit and found Rachel standing in his way, her own pistol raised.

"You can't leave," she said. "I've already called for backup. And yes, we know the FBI surveils this property. They're aware of our efforts to find the last Nazis. You being one of them."

"Do you know who I am?"

"I know stories of you. I know you worked for us. I know you just killed an Israeli diplomat."

Mr. Mortimer strode closer. "Then you know I'm not your enemy."

"Stop!"

Mr. Mortimer stepped forward again.

"I'll shoot."

"You may. I'll survive. I'll kill you. It's worthless for you to die, too."

She lifted the pistol and leveled it at his head.

"What makes you think you'll survive if other men could not kill me?" He smiled and raised his hands to shoulder level in faux surrender.

She gritted her teeth. "What makes you think today can't be that day?"

Mr. Mortimer lifted his glasses to brow level. "I suppose I don't. I'm sorry. I'll do as you say."

For 75 years, people all reacted the same way.

As Rachel caught her breath, Mr. Mortimer smacked the handgun from her grasp with shocking force. "They never trained you for a man like me. I don't want to hurt you."

Frozen, Rachel asked, "What are you?"

"A machine made by hate." Mortimer stepped closer. "Fueled by the lives of the innocent," he snapped. His voice grew louder. "Driven by the revenge of all concerned."

Rachel turned to flee, but in an instant Mr. Mortimer whipped off his belt and lashed it out. It cracked in the air and snared her by the neck. He yanked her into his grasp. His fingers dug deep through her flesh, pinched her muscles, and squeezed her joints. "I know your people. I know their ways. They would have another exit. Show me now. I have no hate for you."

The remaining security guard posted at the door hurled a tactical knife at Mr. Mortimer, stabbing him deep in the breast.

Mr. Mortimer considered the knife in his chest with curious interest. Blood was slow to spread. "Cute," he scoffed as he removed the steel from his flesh without flinching. He dropped the knife to the ground and slackened the belt from Rachel's neck. "There's been enough hostility for today. I will not harm you. Please."

Rachel stared at the knife wound in disbelief. "Fine," Rachel relented, with a shaken, zoned-out blink. "This way. There's a door that leads to other buildings on the block. A prohibition tunnel." She loosened the leather strap further but walked in submission.

Rachel wound through the abandoned kitchen. Directed Mr. Mortimer to a basement door, which she opened into darkness. She then reached for a light switch.

"That won't be necessary," he said.

"All the better." She pivoted and sent a Krav Maga front kick out to Mr. Mortimer.

He blocked the attack and caught her leg, then delivered a breaking blow to her knee before hurling her down the dark stairs like a rag doll.

The remaining security guard dashed from behind. He drew his firearm and fired in rapid succession.

Mr. Mortimer heard him at the first steps. Anticipating the attack, he turned and countered with an animalistic attack.

In what lasted less than a minute, Mortimer said over the smashed man, "For a country who used me as their killer, they should have brought more soldiers for my funeral."

The guard strained for final breaths. With a broken neck, he struggled to shake his head in a frantic attempt for mercy as Mr. Mortimer's foot flashed down to his skull.

Chapter Eighteen

Mr. Mortimer emerged from a connected service tunnel to a Chinese restaurant. He exited reading a Mandarin newspaper, wearing Saul's jacket. His gait toward the bus stop was deliberate but unassuming. A bullet had struck and remained in his body. Soon, scar tissue would envelop it like a small cyst. Bleeding had slowed after Mortimer wrapped it with dingy chef's aprons long discarded on the dusty basement shelves. The wound affected him no more than a rash.

Black vehicles converged on the Mossad front company deli as Mr. Mortimer stepped onto the Pace bus and had his transfer ticket punched. It had been a setup all along. Saul. The war criminals. Yitzhak's loyalty. Self-survival over blood ties.

He walked to the back of the bus and sat down, focused on the scene beyond the wide windows. Isolated for most of his life, he was never more alone.

Black-clad men swarmed the building; Israeli, German, or American, he did not know. Either would want him taken or executed. The world needed its monsters—so they could kill them in the spotlight.

A puberty-cracking voice from behind his seat said, "It's

taken." The tone had a strong intent, but not enough hostility to worry Mr. Mortimer. It was a young bully, not a killer.

He ignored the statement and focused on the bus map posted in the upper corner. He knew the bus number wasn't his usual and his board choice was a schedule of convenience coming from Cicero Avenue's southern parts, which included a town called Lincolnwood. It was along this swath of territory, approximately ten square miles, where the peaceful town of Skokie had seen a heightened number of crime stats. Despite that, this was a good middle-class economic area full of diverse people who got along.

"Hey, old fart. Get up. This is our area," the voice said again.

Mr. Mortimer twisted to assess the threat.

A young teen laughed. "Nice glasses. You think you're the Terminator, or what?"

The kid sat with his friends, both in hoodies and sweatpants, with hair that looked like a wilting shrub. The one in an olive-green hoodie added, "Go sit down there." He pointed to seats mid-bus.

Mr. Mortimer hadn't paid much attention to a thirty, maybe forty-something year old Hasidic man sitting a few seats away, a common sight in this town. Adorned in a traditional dark suit with a white shirt, black-brimmed hat, beard, and two tangling tassels of curled hair hung just over the ear, the Hasid motioned to Mr. Mortimer with a small hand wave to come and sit.

A shrubhead with a black hood over his head said, "See, your boyfriend wants you to sit with him."

Mr. Mortimer had few options if he wanted to lie low, rest his body, and keep away from law enforcement or foreign enforcers. He turned back to the boys, and one of them swung and struck him across the face, launching his glasses into the air and sending them skidding across the bus floor. While caught by surprise, he still kept enough presence of mind to close his eyes. This was neither the time nor the place to be remembered.

The squeaky kid laughed. "Holy crap, you smacked the hell out of that old Jew bag."

The other boys high-fived each other.

"Now move," green hoodie said. "Old men down to the right."

Mr. Mortimer heard the old voices in his head. The tinny monotone orders from the camps. *"Old men and women. Children. All to the right. Healthy men and women to the left."* The dogs barked over the loudspeaker instructions. Tower lights lit the field's center, where the cold and tired stood in long lines. Shadows like black waters surrounded a small flat island of dirt where they huddled. Tall brick silos glowed brightly against the night. Mr. Mortimer kept his eyes closed, but they couldn't keep out the haunting sounds. The wet cold. The paralyzing fear. He felt a firm push. At first, he thought it was a camp guard nudging him forward.

"Dude, we said get out," one of the three said.

"That will be enough, boys," said a voice from the front of the bus. "Here are your glasses, sir."

Mr. Mortimer felt a gentle hand touch on his arm and something plastic at his fingertips.

He grasped the frames and put them back on. When he opened his eyes, he wasn't the least bit surprised to see the Hasid before him.

"Please, come down with me."

"Yeah, you two lovers go sit," black hood said.

The Hasid glared at the young men.

"What are you going to do about it, Rabbi?"

The Hasid smiled at the kids. "There is a saying. Fear nothing, fear no one, but God Himself. Love every Jew, and every man, as you love yourself."

"That's stupid. Here's a saying," squeaky rebuked and spat on the man of faith.

The Hasid kicked the boy's crotch with the speed and strength of a 50-yard field goal attempt. He backhand slapped the kid on his right, then swung open-handed to his left, striking another boy's cheek with a powerful *crack*. The motions were deliberate but tempered. Enough to stop, but not enough to injure.

He said, "It is stupid. But I take personal responsibility for my fellow man. Lesson complete."

The other boys said and did nothing.

The man reached for Mr. Mortimer's hand. "If you care to sit with me, sir, I can ensure you get to where you are going safely. I know a little karate and can protect you. You're safe by my side."

Mr. Mortimer took the man's hand and stood. "I have to get off at the next stop, but thank you."

The man's face wrinkled and nose flared as if catching wind of an odd smell from the old man. Still, he shared a friendly smile.

As the bus slowed, Mr. Mortimer stuffed two small white folded paper envelopes into the man's hand. The bundle was rubber banded but still gave a faint rattle from something inside.

The Hasid looked curiously at the bespeckled man before him.

Mortimer patted the man's hand. "A gift. Don't open it here," he said. "One is for you to share with your community, and the other goes to the education center on Woods Drive. Shalom." He stepped off the bus and sighed heavily as he watched the young men still on the bus, now subdued. Still, one flipped Mr. Mortimer the middle finger.

"So much hate," he said, peeking inside his jacket at the wound dressing.

～

Dwight leaned over the family room couch, staring out the window. When the mailman approached the home to stuff the letterbox full of ads, bills, and more bills, Dwight lowered his scuba mask and dove onto the cushions.

"Mommmmm. Mr. sad man. Mailman. Is here. He's. Very yellow. Today." Dwight rolled off the couch and sprung up to the window, startling the mailman. Dwight smiled from under the mask and waved a hand. "Magic. Now you're. Not sad."

The man's surprise turned to a warm smile. He called through the storm window. "Hi, Dwight. I'm not sad when I see you."

"Are you? Ready. For the big. Hug?"

"You bet," the mailman responded.

Dwight burst through the door and squeezed his arms around the man, who bent to greet him.

"Always good to see you, Dwight."

"Buttwipe," Aaron said from behind the door frame.

The mailman broke a small smile, waved, and turned for the next house. "I'll be seeing you tomorrow, Dwight."

"Buttwipe," Aaron harassed again.

Dwight opened his arms. "I can. Give you. A big hug. Too, Aaron."

Aaron pushed Dwight in the face, slamming his head into the door. "Keep your butt hands off me."

Dwight shrugged and skipped through the house, calling, "Mommm. I did it. Again. I changed him. The mail. Man. His yellow got bright. Bright like. The sun. But it went. Away." Dwight frowned. "My. Superpower. Needs. More power."

"Your father comes home today," Esther called from the kitchen. "You don't want him to see you jumping on the couch or wearing your scuba mask. And he really won't want to hear you two fighting."

Dwight stopped skipping.

"Yes!" Aaron's fist pumped the air. "Back in the room you go, bro." He laughed.

"Aaron, that's enough!" she scolded him.

Dwight dropped to sit on a small, plush swivel chair in the sitting room. He kicked the chair around in circles, spinning slowly. "It's not a scuba. Mask. It's my super. Hero. Costume," he muttered. "I'm going. To use. My super. Power. On Dad. So he can't. Hit."

"Good luck with that," Aaron said. He flicked Dwight in the head.

"Aaron. You stop. Now." Dwight's eyes narrowed.

Aaron ignored the warning. He took two pillows from the couch and rushed his older brother, battering him.

Dwight toppled over with the chair and hit his head on an end table. He closed his eyes, absorbing the pain.

Aaron stepped to Dwight, straddling his older brother's head between his legs, then dropped. All his weight fell onto Dwight's chest.

Dwight winced in pain, his head throbbing.

Aaron dug his little nails into little stinging pinches.

"Stop!" Dwight pleaded. His arms were trapped.

"Or what, buttwipe?" Aaron leered forward, jutting his jaw. "Do it. Hit me. So I can kill you."

Dwight's arm wiggled out and snapped up. He seized Aaron by the throat and gave a python-like squeeze.

Aaron's eyes went wide in surprise.

Dwight pulled his brother down while he leaned up to Aaron's ear, his grip growing tighter. "Zayde says. Family. Can go. In a. Snap." With that, Dwight kissed his kid brother on the cheek and smiled, letting his grip relax. "Your colors. Changed. They were prettier. When I. Squeezed. Your neck."

Tears streamed down Aaron's flushed cheeks. He rubbed his throat and took deep, exaggerated breaths. "I'm telling Dad. Right when he gets home. You're going to be locked back in your room where you should be, killer. I'm going to make sure you never get out and they never feed you, so you starve."

Dwight dropped his head back to the carpet floor and grimaced. "I miss. Zayde." He pulled off the diving mask as he got up and started sloughing to the kitchen when something outside caught his eye in the window. "Mom," he whispered. "The monster. He's back."

Chapter Nineteen

"Stay here, boys. Do not come outside. Aaron, watch your brother."

"Whatever." Aaron scuffed his feet along the way to the window. "The monster Dwight said hurt Dad?"

Esther hopped down the front steps of the house toward the stranger. "Excuse me. Can you please stop?"

Mr. Mortimer continued on his path.

"Hey. Sir, excuse me." Esther reached for the stranger's shoulder, but he turned and caught her hand before she could touch him. Her hand was child-like in his large, firm grasp.

"No, excuse me." His voice was deep. Direct. Frosty. "May I help you?"

Esther glared at the old man. Who wore dark sunglasses on such a dreary day? She looked down at the man's formidable hand and snatched hers back. She caught a whiff of something horrible in the air, sending a sharp wave of nausea through her body.

"Forgive me," he said. "I just noticed it's bruised. Did I *hurt* you?"

"No." Esther clutched her wrist, then pulled her sleeve down to her hand. "I hit it on the counter."

Mr. Mortimer turned and strolled away.

"Wait."

He stopped.

"Did you carry my son? He said he saw you down the street and doesn't know how he got home." She stepped toward the old man. He was tall, thin, and weathered, if that was such a description. A scarecrow looming from his perch, perhaps. His confidence was imposing, not his actual structure. "I'm sorry. No, you couldn't have," she corrected herself.

Mr. Mortimer turned to face his neighbor once more. "Am I too old?"

"No. I didn't mean that."

He took a step toward her. "Because I hate children?"

"Oh, no. I never..."

"Well, I do. Keep them away from me. Good day." He turned away.

"Oh, my God. You hate...kids?"

"I don't discriminate. I'm not very fond of you either, Miss." He stopped his departure and turned, catching her eye. "Or your drinking habits while watching an angel."

Aghast at the remark, she snapped her arms into a fold. "I do not have drinking habits." Her voice was indignant at the accusation.

"You're...unclean. I smelled the wine...seeping...from your pores...as soon as you walked out the door. Cheap chardonnay," he sneered.

Her veneer crumbled.

"You buy it because you argue it's kosher, but in truth, you can pay little without your husband taking notice." Mr. Mortimer glanced at a fading bruise on her wrist. He softened, "Or perhaps he just...doesn't care. I'm sorry."

"You're talking to the monster?" Dwight asked.

Esther spun to find Dwight right behind her, Aaron behind him.

"I told you to stay inside!" Her shout ended with a tremor. She grabbed her own hand to stop the shaking.

"Buttwipe wouldn't listen. He's too stupid," said Aaron.

Embarrassed by her outburst and son, she looked over her shoulder.

The old man was looming right behind her.

She jumped. "Oh, my God!"

Dwight guffawed. His laugh wasn't contagious.

Aaron gave the creepy old man more than a cautious side-eyed assessment. He grabbed his mother's hand. "I want to go." He tugged at her with a look of desperation. "Now."

Mr. Mortimer squatted down next to Dwight and extended his hand. "I'm Mr. Mortimer."

"Mr. Monster." Dwight rushed to give Mr. Mortimer a bear hug.

"Oh, my God. Dwight. No! He hates..."

Mr. Mortimer enveloped Dwight in a tight embrace. "I told you, this is the angel."

Esther squinted, then bent further for a better look at the blue-inked tattoo on the man's lower forearm, peeking from his coat.

"The 'Z' before the numbers." She pulled from Aaron. Esther pointed to Mr. Mortimer's arm with a look of revelation. "Of course. From his stories. You're the Gypsy."

"Romani," he corrected politely.

"You knew my father-in-law. It *was* you."

"We shared history."

Dwight broke from the embrace with a smile. He reached for Mr. Mortimer's glasses but was warned with a wagging finger. "When my. Daddy. Comes home. You need. To protect us. Again. Right? But. Don't break. My room or. My dad. Again."

Esther cocked her head.

Aaron shoved his brother hard to the ground. "Don't talk about that. This old man didn't do it. He's old like Zayde, and stupid. He can't even lift a cane. He'll probably be dead soon."

Esther struggled with where to focus her attention. She knelt to help Dwight, who was crying from the hard fall.

Mr. Mortimer focused on Aaron. He raised a hand to his glasses and bent down toward the boy. "I'll see you soon." He exposed his black eyes as the boy stood in shock. "O shoshoy kaste si feri yek khiv sigo athadjol." *The rabbit with only one hole is soon caught,* he translated in a whisper.

Aaron covered his ears in terror and closed his eyes.

I'm in your head. I will be in your house. And I will send you falling into a deep, dark, tight hole. I will snare you, little rabbit, or bury you where you live.

Chapter Twenty

By the time Rabbi Dratch brought David home from the hospital, the boys were in their rooms. Aaron had been inconsolable for the rest of the afternoon and early evening but wouldn't say why. He'd gone straight to his room and locked the door after giving Dwight an unwarranted punch in the gut. As Esther banged on the door, demanding an apology, Aaron screamed he wasn't sorry and wouldn't come out until his father was back home.

Dwight, on the other hand, was now in an exceptional mood, despite the punch, and had been dancing around the house with the mask and snorkel until his mom thought it best for him to go back into his room. Father would be home soon, she warned. To herself, she also warned, *He'll be home soon.*

"Let him know. Mr. Monster came. To say. Hi," Dwight sang as he pranced up the stairs.

Esther tuned out the world at that moment. Like a zombie, she walked to the kitchen and without warning felt a wave of nausea scorching her insides. She barely made it to the bathroom before her anguish exploded. Her body trembled as wave after wave passed. The cold porcelain at her ankles was a small comfort as she relived the horrific sights and sounds of her own monster at home.

Esther read a proverb on the wall. It had no place in the powder room, but her father-in-law had hung it there. *He that can't endure the bad, will not live to see the good.*

"Did you see enough of the good before you endured more bad?" she whispered to herself, as if Yitzhak was there.

She tried to collect herself and washed cold water on her face and arms. She then returned to the kitchen, where she poured herself a glass of wine to the rim and gulped it down. She poured another one and swallowed as fast as she could, hoping the numbness would arrive faster. On her third pour, she walked to the sitting room and sat in wait. Like Dwight, she swirled the chair around. Nervous. Vulnerable. Scared. Hopeless.

Across the room stood on a shelf a small framed picture. The word "Family" was etched into the stainless steel. Within it was a sun-bleached image of Esther and her sister, Beth, both of them arm and arm during a snapshot of Esther's undergraduate ceremony. Both smiling. They'd been inseparable. A happy moment of a time gone but haunting each day.

"Whore," Esther accused her aloud and flipped the picture over on its face. "I have no family. No friends. No faith." She downed the rest of the glass and set it on top of the frame. "And I don't give a fu-"

David walked through the door.

Esther turned to his entrance and felt the heat building again in her entrails. Her mouth dried, and her temples and nose sweat. She mustered a welcoming embrace for appearances, stumbling along the way.

He pushed down her arms and turned away. "Sleep it off on the couch. I'm going up to bed."

David's face was bandaged. Bruised. His stitches buckled under the swelling. He held a small plastic bag with prescriptions and instructions in his hand. Not turning or taking off his shoes, he lumbered to the stairs like his feet wore cement blocks.

"Goodnight, Rabbi Dratch." His speech was soft and broken as his body looked. "Thanks for the ride, and your advice."

"My pleasure, David. Get some good sleep. Take your medicine." Rabbi Dratch frowned at Esther. The man of God nodded his head toward the sitting room sofa, pursing his lips. "Please call me if I can be of further help."

Before Esther could utter a word, Rabbi Dratch turned to leave, saying, "Just give him some time to recover. Perhaps a week with you on the sofa will give him some rest." He stopped and twisted his head back with more unsolicited advice. "Keep the boys playing outside, so as not to disturb him. Just be a good wife. Run the household. A wounded ego can take longer to mend than a broken body. You can help him with a clean and pious home. It should be your honor. The old adage, 'a nice wife, a nice house, and nice dishes.' Have some more tolerance for him in the next few days."

Esther rubbed her face with her hands, biting her lower lip. She inhaled with her nose pillowed in her hot, sweaty palms. Her hands dropped. Her jaw slackened. She was careful not to slur. The wine was already dancing with needled heels across her face.

"Rabbi. Please. I must speak with you."

"Esther. There is no need for talk. He's a good man. Remember the Sermon on the Mount. Turn to him the other cheek if he might slap it. Perhaps make some coffee. Have yourself a bite to eat before you check on him. Goodnight."

Dwight was still awake when he heard his father's footfalls at the top of the stairs. The sound of small steps grew closer to the door. Dwight heard the tinny clink of the door knob.

The dread of his father's return fell hard as reality set in. He was long past dancing as he lay alone in the dark. Paint and plaster fumes still assaulted his nose days after repair. Dwight trembled and pulled his covers tight above his head. He wished he'd gone to the bathroom one last time. The pressure down below grew. While his eyes were closed, they burned.

The latch clicked. The knob released. And the rehung door creaked under protest.

Dwight released his bladder. "I'm sorry," he mouthed and flipped over in his wetness, burying his face in the pillow. Waiting. When the hand touched his back, he whispered, "Monster."

~

A aron awoke hours later in the darkness from the bed's shuttering, as if a slight earthquake held the bunks. The tremors were jarring enough that he grabbed the sides of the mattress.

"Dad?"

The shaking stopped.

Then started again.

A deep voice spoke from under Aaron's top bunk. "I'm here, Rabbit. If you call for your dad, I'll kill him."

The bed shook again.

Aaron cried. He bit the edge of his blanket.

Something touched his feet.

Rabbit.

Aaron drew his legs up as high as he could, holding his knees in desperation. Shaking.

Rabbit.

The covers moved down from his body. With one hand, he grabbed the receding covers and gripped with all his might. Still, they were being pulled down to the end of the bed. Aaron grabbed them with his other hand in terror. Both fists were now full of fabric, tugging and losing the battle as the sheets and blankets slid from his body.

The voice spoke again. "Do you have to pee? Can you feel the pressure, Rabbit? If you pee, I'll rip off your legs and make you chew off your toes. The doctors will have to rip open your stomach to get them out. Is it building in you? The fear, Rabbit?"

A hand reached over the side of the mattress and pawed at Aaron's side. He scrambled to the wall.

Another hand slid up the wall to where he huddled and pinched at anything it could grab.

In agony, Aaron fought the mounting bladder pressure. Sweat cascaded down his back, his breathing hyper. The long shadows separating from the shades of darkness in the room seemed to come for him. Tears rolled down the sides of his face and pooled under his lids.

"Why do you treat your brother with such hate, Rabbit?"

After a long silence, Aaron whimpered, "I don't know."

"You know. Tell me."

The bed shook. The hands seemed to be everywhere, coming from the sides, the foot, and the top of the bed.

Aaron was hyperventilating. He crossed his legs and reached a hand down to squeeze himself. He knew he couldn't hold it much longer and tried to tighten his insides. A trickle was coming. He wouldn't be able to stop it.

"Answer me." The bed shook from under Aaron again. "I said answer me, Rabbit," the voice growled. A closet door opened and closed. Something large now stood in the shadows, coming for Aaron.

"Because he bothers me."

"Lies, Rabbit. Tell me."

"Because everyone likes him except my dad."

"Why don't they like you?"

"I don't know."

The mattress lifted, then flopped back down. "You know."

Aaron sniveled. "Because I'm mean."

"Mean like your father, you little turd."

The pee was coming soon. He couldn't stop it.

"I'm watching you, Rabbit. I'm listening out for you. I see everything and hear everything. Next time I come back, you'll just disappear. Down the hole. And I'll cover you in it. Upside down. Dead Rabbit."

Aaron squealed and released his bladder, crying silently.

Mr. Mortimer seized the opening in Aaron's mind where extreme fear meant the subconscious released its worldly grip.

I know all your thoughts. I live in your head. I'll be back, Rabbit.

❧

David tossed and turned in fitful sleep. His bruised and battered body kept him from respite despite the drugs. He was exhausted. Anxiety awoke him, and every shadow in the room reminded him of that night. David got up from bed and flipped on the light switch near the bedroom entrance. For a moment, he questioned Esther's empty spot in the bed.

There were the visions and angst from the attack, but it was the voices that continued to haunt him since his father's death. A voice constantly whispered to him. Haunting him. Calling from beyond.

Back in bed, he flipped from side to side, tangling himself in the sheets. Frustrated, he reached to his nightstand for the bottle of pills. In his delirium, he couldn't recall how many he'd had. It didn't matter. The voices, restlessness, and constant fear had to stop. David reached for the glass of water he'd filled before turning in.

A hand clamped down over his hand with a vise-like squeeze. Another hand tightened around his throat, forcing his head deep into the pillow.

"You're nothing like your father," Mr. Mortimer growled. "Nonetheless, I need something from you. If you can give it, it will be better for me, better for your family."

Chapter Twenty-One

There were two screams of horror the next morning when Esther found the bodies.

Detective Jefferson wasn't greeted with a hug when she entered the Skinner home after the police call that morning. Dwight was, instead, slumped back into the couch, kicking his heels into the chair base while toying in silence with his mask and snorkel. He said nothing and averted his eyes.

As Esther described it to the first responders, the first scream came when she'd entered the master bedroom to check on her husband, only to find him in full rigor mortis. After seeing the note, she rushed into her son's bedroom. Where she screamed again.

"He killed him," was all she could say. Over and over. "He killed him."

Esther flopped down on a chair at the kitchen table with two police officers, then bounced back up, busying herself. She'd made one of the officers coffee, while another nursed from a large Dunkin Donuts cup. Just as quick as she'd made it, Esther poured the coffee down the sink and made another full pot while searching for a box of tea from the shelf.

"Detective," a police officer, Cole Schmidt, addressed

Jefferson with a nod, then pointed to Esther's back, circling a crazy gesture with his hands and head. The Dunkin cop also gave his cursory nod and affirmed with his wide eyes on Esther with his wiggling drinking hand. He turned back after a moment and hot sip. "Detective, the M.E. will be here in a few. Take your time. We're going to get Mrs. Skinner some tea or coffee."

"Thanks." Detective Jefferson looked long and hard at Esther Skinner, who didn't say anything. If the woman had looked like a train wreck before, she now wore the damage of a mile-long fatal car pile-up. "Rodriguez coming back?"

The two cops shook their heads.

"He sounded shaken," the detective said. "I'll head upstairs. I'd like to talk to Mrs. Skinner when you're done speaking with her, please."

The police tape hung loosely on both doors like yellow jump ropes or birthday streamers draped from archways before the big surprise.

Detective Jefferson prepared herself as she ducked under the tape and pushed Aaron's door open. She didn't expect to meet his dead, open eyes engaging hers from the dim closet. His body was suspended by his neck with a long leather belt wrapped around the clothes rod. His bare toes touched the floor, even with his knees bent. He wore briefs and a summer camp T-shirt. His bluish arms were hunched over, and his puffy face was tilted to the side. His mouth was open and loose, as if he were in a dental chair, getting his teeth cleaned.

Nothing else in the room was out of the ordinary save for a mound of bed sheets by the door. The top bunk's mattress was bare. A blanket dangled over the foot rail.

Detective Jefferson pulled a packet of surgical gloves from her pocket and snapped the latex over her wrist. In one hand, she held her iPhone and raised it to her mouth. "God dang it." She scolded the mobile device and liberated a thumb from the glove to press the screen. "Crime scene. Initial thoughts and observations. The youngest Skinner boy, Aaron, deceased."

The detective stopped the recording. She took a deep breath and started again, fighting back the mounting tears. *The kid was a shit, but damn, he was still a kid.*

Detective Jefferson scanned the room again. She expected to see trophies, ribbon participation medals, maybe team photos of Little League and Pee Wee Football. There was just...nothing. *What does this kid do with all his energy?* she asked herself.

She turned to Aaron in the closet. No answers beyond the obvious.

Detective Jefferson tried again. "Hanging in the closet. Child was found unresponsive, not breathing. His body has not been moved. Call to me this mornin' said Mrs. Skinner first found husband, and then boy. She left boy to check on the oldest son, who was unharmed and sleeping. She called police. Likely murder-suicide, but why other than punishment to the wife, who husband already controlled? Why a hanging? No evidence that boy was not suicidal. Did the boy kill himself? Father responded in kind?"

Her phone rang. Her husband. She declined the call but texted: *At a crime scene. Giving you my biggest hugs. So sad. Hope ur having a good week.* She added hearts and a kiss emoji.

Detective Jefferson reached into the bed linen pile, shuffling the fabric around. She lifted a pair of inside-out pajamas with underwear still clinging to the pant legs and leaned in for a cautious sniff.

"Urine soiled clothes found near the door. Very little bodily release in or on clothing post mortem. Question is, did the boy remove the sheets before he was killed, or did the mother remove them, post-mortem?" she recorded. "Youngest son does not strike me as a bedwetter."

Detective Jefferson dropped the pants to the floor and inspected the sheets closer. "Bed sheets also soiled from urine. If suicide was the initial course of action, what instigated it? Who instigated it? Did the husband? Had he been remorseful? Initial contact with family showed the youngest son and husband were tight. Contrary to the rest of the family. Aaron Skinner and husband were likely the abusers of the family. On my prior visit, Esther showed signs of abuse; bruising, sheepish demeanor."

"Is Aaron still dead? I want to see if his colors are there."

Detective Jefferson whipped around to a presence behind her. Seeing Dwight, she ushered the boy out, closing the door behind them.

"Oh, honey." She bent to her knees. "You shouldn't be up here."

"I want to see his colors again." Dwight's eyes narrowed, and he shoved her aside with surprising strength.

"Ma'am!" Detective Jefferson called out to Esther.

Dwight continued to push with incredible strength. The detective grabbed a handful of his pajamas.

Dwight swatted off her hand easily and entered the room, flipping up the yellow tape as he went.

Detective Jefferson called again for help. "Ma'am! Officers!"

Dwight faced his little brother.

The party downstairs scampered up.

Detective Jefferson stepped in front of Dwight, who pushed her aside, again. "Honey, you don't want to see this and remember him this way."

"Oh, God." Esther drew her hand to her mouth. "Dwight, you can't be in here." She stepped close to the detective and bent toward her son. "The colors are gone, baby. Come downstairs."

Dwight grinned. "I know. I saw them. Go. I heard. The whispers. That he was. Gone. For good."

"Monster?" Esther asked.

Dwight shrugged. "Maybe. Maybe not." He lifted a finger to his lips and looked to Detective Jefferson. "Shhh."

Chapter Twenty-Two

Detective Jefferson held her puzzled face as the room cleared. As Dwight was escorted toward the stairs, she called out, "Dwight, what color was your brother?"

Without turning, he said, "Spinach. Blech."

"Green?"

Dwight nodded.

"Dark green? Or hazy, like a cloud over it."

Dwight smiled. "It went. Away."

"Did you help make it go away?"

The boy shrugged and pulled his scuba mask down over his eyes and nose.

"I'll be damned." The detective's phone rang in her hand. She texted a reply instead of answering. *GO AHEAD AND GIVE HIM APPLESAUCE. AND A HUG. COMING BACK EARLY.*

Esther shuffled Dwight out of view. "Go outside and play for a little while."

Detective Jefferson caught Eshter's eye. "Mrs. Skinner, I know it's a loaded question. How are you holding up?"

Esther tightened her lips. She gave a small broken nod.

"I'll be down in a moment. I promise I'll keep it short."

Detective Jefferson gave a small wave that felt inappropriate as soon as she did it. It was time to investigate the husband. The detective reached inside her blazer jacket, touching a Springfield Hellcat pistol nested within a shoulder holster. This place gave her the creeps.

~

The house's master bedroom was dark, and Detective Jefferson backhanded the wall for a light switch as she walked under the police tape to inspect the second body. If it hadn't been a crime scene, she would have been afraid of waking the man lying peacefully in bed. In the light, the bluish lips snitched David Skinner's true disposition. As far as the detective was concerned, he was a hitter, and she felt little for the corpse before her, save for a sliver of contempt.

She stood for a while, trying to envision David as her own husband. Things were never easy, but they were never bad. Rodger, her own husband, would never even consider putting hands on her. He could never harm their children. There was love in their home. Chaos, but love. Pictures, awards, recognition saying, *We see you as an individual. We see ourselves as a family. We work for each other. We work together. We're a unit. Part of a family. A greater family and a community.* That was the difference. That was everything.

Detective Jefferson returned mentally to her craft. Just as Rodriguez had said on the phone, there it lay on the nightstand. A handwritten note with three simple words.

"I hate you."

Clear but not convincing. Detective Jefferson had seen murder-suicide cases like this before. I can't love myself and want to hurt everyone else so they know my pain.

She asked herself, *How is it Dwight remained unharmed if the husband wanted to hurt his wife? Yes, Dwight could have killed his brother, but hanging him? Esther probably didn't have the strength. Would Dwight have been capable of overdosing his father with pills? Certainly not.* The simplest explanation was usually the reality.

The detective meandered around the room, looking for something telling.

On the floor were some small bits of yard debris. Detective Jefferson bent to examine them. Blade of grass, a little dirt, part of a leaf.

The family left their shoes by the front door.

She peeked around the bed. David's shoes. She turned the shoes over. In the small grooves, grass, a little dirt.

Bastard. I'm trying to help you. Help me, David. How do you go from getting clobbered to killing your son and yourself? The detective remained puzzled. *No one in this home could have beaten up the husband. Dwight?*

It was in the hallway where she first paid attention to the latch and lock on the outside of Dwight's bedroom door. Movement below the stairs caught her eye. Dwight was twirling down on the main level.

The boy with the scuba mask who hugs people and sees their colors? Like auras. Can he see their true colors? Is he capable?

Detective Jefferson stepped into Dwight's room. It was cleaned and repaired. On the walls were taped pieces of paper. She stepped closer to look at the crayon colorings.

Chapter Twenty-Three

When the detective came back downstairs, Dwight was sitting with his mother.

"Hun, is there anywhere Dwight can go while we talk?"

Esther patted Dwight's back. "He'll be fine outside for a while. He just needs a minute."

"I mean, any family that can come get him?" Detective Jefferson sat on the corner of the sofa and ran her fingers through Dwight's thick hair as he rolled a Matchbox car over his legs.

Esther's eyes zeroed in on the detective's caress.

Detective Jefferson pulled back her hand. "I'm sorry. I overstepped. I couldn't help it. That's just the mom in me."

Esther blushed. "Not at all. It's why he likes you. You have a good heart, Detective." Esther exhaled. "To answer your question. First of many, I'm guessing, we have no one else."

"A friend? No family at all?"

Esther's discomfort was palpable. "It's been hard." She scratched her son's back as he continued the driving route up her leg, detouring up her torso between her breasts, under her chin, over her mouth, and stopped at her nose. The car made a slow one-eighty and took the same path back.

Esther wiped at her eyes. "He doesn't need to be shielded from anything." She watched him play and sniffed with a smile. "We've seen a lot of death. I think he understands it better than any of us. It's part of the history we carry." Esther filled her lungs again and exhaled a lifetime of loss. "What do you want to know?"

"May I?" Detective Jefferson indicated to the other sofa closer to Esther.

"Of course." Esther asked, "Would you like some coffee? I made some not too long ago. It's fresh." Esther popped up. "I have tea, too. I found a few boxes I never even knew I had until today." She laughed nervously. "I don't even drink Chamomile," she said, then bit her lip. "My mother-in-law did," Esther choked out, tears falling free. "I have decaf. Oh, my God. I can't even think. I just have so much-"

"Mrs. Skinner. Really, I'm good. Small bladder." Detective Jefferson pointed to her abdomen. "One kidney. What can you do? Come sit."

Esther touched her own chest. Surprised by the comment. "Oh. I'm sorry."

"Don't be. My decision. I gave it to my husband. We're a match." She smiled with pride before realizing the tactless comment. "I'm sorry. I was just trying to-"

"I understand. It's okay." Esther lowered her head. "Dwight, please be a good boy. Go on outside for a little bit so Mommy can talk with her friend."

As if he'd thought of it on his own, Dwight asked, "Can I. Go outside?"

"Yes, sweetie." Dwight gave his mom a hug, then tilted his head so he could kiss her without bumping her with his mask. Anything but rude, Dwight opened his arms wide for an embrace from the detective, which she obliged.

"I'm going. Outside," he said.

"Okay," the moms replied in unison and smiled.

"He's a special little boy. I can tell firsthand."

"You have no idea."

The detective pulled a small notepad from her purse. "Do you mind if we continue?"

"Actually, I have a question for you, Detective."

Chapter Twenty-Four

Before the question could leave her mouth, Esther burst into tears for the second time in minutes. She tried deep breaths, even stomped her feet and pounded her legs with her fists. Still, expressing what was bottled up inside just couldn't be articulated. She pulled at her hair, balling her hands in the strands.

Whether it was professional or appropriate, woman-to-woman, Detective Jefferson pulled Esther in close until their heads met. "Can I try saying what I think you're going to ask?" Feeling Esther's head scrape up and down against her own told the detective it was okay. "Maybe you're devastated about your son while feeling perhaps free from your husband?"

Esther's head movement confirmed it.

"He was a hitter, wasn't he?"

Again, the movement.

"And he took it out on Dwight, too. That right?"

Esther nodded.

"Maybe now you're feeling all alone, and not even that old rabbi can help because he's just as blind and old school as everyone else has been around you."

Esther sniffed hard. She pulled a wadded-up Kleenex from her dress pocket and opened it for a thick blow. With welled eyes, she set her attention to Detective Jefferson. "No one cared. No one listened. David took everything from me. My life, my career, my sister."

"What happened to your sister?"

Esther remained silent until, detective moniker aside, Stacy Jefferson gave her a reassuring tug. "It's just us girls. I won't note that."

"They had an affair. At least I thought they did. I mean, she always had it easy. Never had a problem with attracting men," she said, with a knowing look. "And she liked to...flirt. Wasn't opposed to kissing a married man. Turned out she got herself in one of those situations with my husband." Ether's nostrils flared. She huffed her long held frustrations. "David forced himself on my sister when he helped her move out of a downtown apartment to Evanston. I couldn't go. I was pregnant. I blamed her. I felt like it was her fault. One night when David was working late, Dwight and I went to see her. She and I had a heart-to-heart, and I found out the truth." Esther choked back tears. "While Dwight was playing," she shrugged, "my sister and I got drunk. We got in an accident. The car rolled." Esther paused. "Dwight got hurt. She was killed."

"I'm sorry."

Esther used her sleeve to wipe her eyes. "My parents blamed me. For all of it. Said I wasn't being dutiful."

"And where are they?"

"Buried. Florida." Esther sniffed hard. "Hurricane statistic. I mean, it happens. It's on the news. But who really knows someone who dies?" Esther started sobbing again. "It follows us. Death. Everywhere."

Detective Jefferson blew out the weight of the situation. "And now your husband took one of the very last of the family you love."

Esther nodded.

"Why do you think he left Dwight if he was already hitting him?"

"To punish me. To leave me with Dwight to care for all by myself. He hated that little angel. Hated me for loving him. He even turned Aaron on us because of that hate. I wouldn't end the pregnancy. This is that bastard's last word."

"I understand. Esther, can I ask you one last thing? It's going to sound ridiculous."

Esther's brows rose in concern, but she nodded.

"Did you have anything to do with the deaths of your husband or Aaron?"

Aghast, Esther looked stunned. In the next moment, she sprung up from the sofa and stepped back from the detective. "Get out of my house. Get out!" Esther pointed to the door and caught sight of something outside through the window. "Oh, no. Dwight! Stop!"

Chapter Twenty-Five

Dwight sat on the sidewalk, legs folded crisscross applesauce style, with Mr. Mortimer, who was doing the same.

Esther burst from the door, Detective Jefferson following close behind. "Dwight, get in the house. What are you doing with my son?"

Mr. Mortimer rose and gave a slight bow. "Mrs. Skinner, my condolences. I was out for a walk, saw the police cars and your son outside, and thought I'd see if you all were okay." He nodded toward Dwight. "I hope I didn't overstep. The little fellow looked like he could use a friend."

Detective Jefferson was hot on her heels. "Mrs. Skinner, do you know this man? Is it okay?"

Esther bit her lip. "I don't know. Just leave. It's fine."

Dwight giggled. "My. Monster."

"Dwight! It's Mr. Mortimer. Can't you just give me a break for a minute?!" Esther's eyes bulged with embarrassment before she closed them. "I'm so sorry."

"Admittedly, Mr. Mortimer's just what people tend to call me. It stuck even for me. Mort Eiserman." He extended a hand to the detective. "Monster, not so much."

Detective Jefferson shook his hand and stared at the man's dark glasses. It was a rather cloudy, overcast day. Was it cataracts old people wore those glasses for? She couldn't recall.

"He's a neighbor," Esther informed the detective.

"Yitzhak Skinner, the house patriarch, was a dear friend. I knew his son since he was at my knee." Mr. Mortimer smiled. "We were...drinking buddies." He paused at Esther's curious reaction. "Yitzhak. Not his son." Mr. Mortimer pulled up his sleeve, showing the detective and Esther, once again, his faded blue Auschwitz prisoner tattoo.

Mr. Mortimer turned toward home. "Come visit me, Dwight, if your mother says it's okay. That goes for you, too, Mrs. Skinner. Please feel free to come by if I can ever help or assist with any arrangements. I'm retired, you know. We can sit by the fire and talk. Like family."

Detective Jefferson tread with caution. "Is...this something you're comfortable with?" Her face showed more than a degree of apprehension.

Before Esther could answer, Dwight nodded, with a smile. "He killed. My daddy. And Aaron. It got. Whispered. To me."

Chapter Twenty-Six

Again, Esther ushered Dwight away from the detective. "I need to get him some lunch."

"Bye," Dwight called back. "I love you. My mom's. Police. Friend."

The two police officers exited the home. "Detective," the Dunkin Donuts drinker called out, waiting to continue once the wife had closed the door. "The M.E. is on his way. Do you even want them in the house? I mean, it's still a crime scene. Are you finished?"

Out of her element, and clearly out of control, she waved off. "Yeah, I'm finished. We'll let the M.E. confirm what we're all thinking anyway, but I want him to examine ligature strangulation versus smothering on the boy. Need to confirm mechanical asphyxia."

"Roger, that," the officer replied. "Did you get that?" he asked his partner.

Detective Jefferson thought now might be a good time to call her own husband and say hello. She thought better of it when the rabbi pulled up.

She marched up to Dratch as he exited his car. "Oh no, you don't. Nu-uh. Not today, Rabbi. This isn't a block party."

"Detective Jefferson. How amusing, as always," he said.

Detective Jefferson didn't budge. "No. Mrs. Skinner is not taking visitors. I still have an active crime scene and don't need any evidence tampered."

"I'm not here to see Mrs. Skinner. I'm here to ensure the deceased are handled according to our traditions."

The detective paused. "Well, unless you have a Jewish handbook for me to read, you're gonna have to let me Google that one for a minute before I let you in."

The rabbi stepped aside and continued walking up the drive, with no apparent intention of heeding the detective's request. "As you know, I work with the department. Take it up with your boss, Detective. You may wish to phone him instead of Googling. I know I plan to. I'll give you a head start."

"No." Detective Jefferson rushed up from behind, grabbed the man's arm, and stuck a finger at his face. It wasn't the first time the detective had stopped a man with one finger, but today was an exception as Rabbi Dratch swatted away her hand and proceeded.

She grabbed his arm and pulled him right back around.

"You did *not* help that woman when she needed help. You did not create a safe place for that woman or that child, and you knew he was a hitter. You goddamned knew it the whole time, and now a little boy is dead."

Detective Jefferson lowered her voice and tried to calm herself when Dwight and Esther appeared behind the front picture window.

Dratch fumed. "As you have just gone outside of your jurisdiction and law, I will no longer address you as a detective. In Jewish tradition, wives are expected to perform specific tasks to serve their husbands. Disrespectful women may at times need to be reminded of their place, just like children. Just as a lion may tear flesh with no shame, so may the man of a bad wife who fails to perform according to Jewish law. What you consider beating is biblical chastisement to educate and train. This woman needs training."

"Motherfucker, you did *not* just say that in front of me."

"Perhaps you need an education, too."

Detective Jefferson balled her fists.

"I think that was enough education for one day, Moshe," said Mr. Mortimer. Neither the detective nor rabbi knew where he came from, as both were startled with a fearful jolt and shudder. Mr. Mortimer showed a toothy grin. "Rabbi, the deceased are not alone. Nor have they been since the moment of death. From what I have been told, there is no blood to be gathered. The remains are intact. According to the traditions, there will be no autopsy." Mr. Mortimer let that sink in with the detective, then continued. "I am sure Mrs. Skinner can opt out of a post-mortem examination, but ultimately the medical examiner, not you, will make that determination. The honor of the dead has been preserved, and we would hate for you to become unclean by handling the bodies in any way. Please leave, as your religious services are not required."

"He said you would come," the rabbi hissed in a slow, non-confrontational manner.

"And so I have." Mr. Mortimer gave a slight bow.

Chapter Twenty–Seven

The rabbi looked to the detective for comment.

"He's not involved. Don't listen to him," Dratch said.

Detective Jefferson was still figuring out what exactly was going on in this odd little town rife with secrets and silence, and how this old man had just blurted out procedurals chapter and verse but was also accused of being a murderer by a child. The evidence pointed to murder-suicide.

Mr. Mortimer took another step toward Dratch. "The detective and I have already become acquainted. Introduced by Esther."

"Does she know it was you?" the rabbi asked in nothing less than an accusatory tone.

"Careful, my friend. The detective may take your words out of context. It would be unfortunate for everyone here to cause any confusion."

The rabbi's machismo and self-righteousness had long ago evaporated in the moment. He drew closer to the detective. "Have you seen his eyes? Such that it would appear of no eyes at all. Dark hollows in his head. He is the one I spoke of. The supernatural one who is the whisperer to the world. This is your suspect. Your killer."

Mr. Mortimer sighed. "Really, you wish for me to endure more pain and suffering. Now I subject myself to embarrassment and your ridicule. As you wish, Rabbi." Mr. Mortimer lifted his dark glasses. "I assure you, despite my friend's accusation, my unique coloring is nothing more than the courtesy of a Nazi madman from a lifetime ago. If he weren't dead, someone should seek to revoke his license to practice."

"Oh, dear God," Detective Jefferson said. Her mouth went wide with horror.

Before her stood the old survivor, his eyes only slits within the scarring of burnt flesh.

Mortimer continued. "Thank you, Rabbi, for allowing me to show the world what heinous crimes of the past I have endured." Mr. Mortimer leaned in to Dratch and sniffed the air. "I can smell your urine...bladder cancer. Focus on yourself. For your own health. Time's ticking." He winked at the Rabbi, then turned. "Detective, please call on me if you wish to interrogate an old man who has spent enough days imprisoned against his will by baseless accusations of the fearful." With that, he walked away.

"He was squinting, so you couldn't see. They are black. He has black eyes," the rabbi said in protest. "Did you not see them? Only the devil himself has black eyes."

"I think what I have seen is you, Rabbi. Your true colors," the detective said. "Time for you to leave. Call the chief. I'm happy to arrest you on the spot, even if it means losing my job. I'll deal with Mr. Mortimer. At present, he is not a suspect."

Mr. Mortimer walked on his way, rechecking his smile while humming away to the sweet songs of Johnny Cash. Far enough out of sight, he removed a small latex burn prosthetic. Nothing a little glue and melted crayons couldn't make. After a glass or two of spirits, it would be time for a rest. He had a very busy evening planned, but first he would need to deal with the tail he could sense behind him. Mossad rarely drove pickup trucks with German death metal music.

As he strolled home, he caught the tip of his shoe on a raised sidewalk slab. He fell hard to his knees and failed to stop the momentum, causing him to scrape his hands and chin.

Detective Jefferson was in her car, following the old man, deciding whether to bring him in for questioning. She was unaware of the truck parked houses away.

She lowered the window and called out as she stopped the vehicle. "Sir, are you okay? Looked like you landed kinda hard."

"I'm fine," he replied, dusting off his palms and pant legs. "I just need a moment for my head to clear."

She leaned further out the window. "Can I give you a ride home? I wouldn't mind asking you a few questions."

Mr. Mortimer winced. "I think I just re-injured my knee and hip. The doctor won't be happy to see me back in rehabilitation. I think I may need to take you up on that offer. Seem to have gotten the wind taken out of me, too."

Detective Jefferson left her car to give Mr. Mortimer support. "That was quite a tumble. You hit your head?"

"I'm not sure. I may have bumped it. I was just so mad. I had to walk away before I said something impolite," he said, then smiled. "You seem like you're very intelligent. I'm sure you're quite good at your job."

"Thank you," she said, helping him into the car. He settled in awkwardly. Stiff. Old.

I n about as long as it took Mr. Mortimer to fasten his seatbelt, they approached his home. "There." He pointed. "The lot behind those tall hedges."

Just outside of the bungalow and split-level style homes that lined the large elm adorned street was a small clearing that snuggled up to a small tree line backdrop and railroad track berm lush with tall grass and cattails. Situated just to the side was a tiny forest of grand arborvitaes that ran the length of a football field on all sides, with a paved drive cutting into the greenery. Just within view over the ten-foot bush tops was a handsome two-story yellow and red trimmed home with a white wraparound porch. Two aqua-blue gables lifted intersecting roof pitches in front of a large chimney. The whole site was both inviting yet out of place among the drab homes leading to the immaculately kept property that exuded a conflicting sense of both privacy and welcome.

It was far from what Detective Jefferson had expected. "That's a lovely home. Is it a historic build? The colors almost make the house glow. It's like a big Gypsy farmhouse."

"Roma. I'm Romani. I prefer that word from *gadjos*. But thank you otherwise for the compliment."

The detective remained transfixed, still unaware of the offensive slang she'd used.

The old man's struggle to get out of the car brought her back to the moment.

"Here, let me come around and help you out. Maybe we can find something in the house to clean you up. You've got a nasty scratch on your chin. Is there anyone home who can help?" She paused. The old man's wound seemed much less dramatic than she recalled.

"I'll be fine. Thank you. It's not easy getting old."

She offered some assistance, lending a hand for support. "Are you sure? I wouldn't mind asking you a few questions. Maybe you can help me figure some things out. You said no one else is home there for you?" Her arm moved around to his back. It felt thicker than he looked. Not bony, as she would have suspected.

"No, I don't think I said that. Let's go to the porch," he said. "We can sit and talk. You can ask your questions. Although, I'm afraid I can't offer much. About as close as I've gotten to that family is from the sidewalk." He walked slowly up a cobblestone walkway. "Do you like bourbon? I can get us a couple glasses, and we can visit for a bit."

"Water would be fine." She gave a tight-lipped smile. Thoughts raced through her head as she continued to reframe perceptions, suspicions, and facts.

"Are you sure? It is a quite interesting spirit. Made by a man of color in Kentucky. Embraced by enthusiasts from the south because of its quality. Colorless judgment. For what it is. On the merits of craftsmanship and the man's character himself. It's as if the young boy, Dwight, taught the lesson. There is so much he could teach the world. The bottle itself is colorful. Almost as if it, too, was telling a story."

The detective nodded at his words. She was distracted. "The boy is special. He seems to like you. Odd thing he said about you, though, don't you think?"

Mr. Mortimer stopped at the porch steps. "Perhaps I didn't hear what he said. Would you care to repeat it?"

She did not. It didn't mean she let it go. As they climbed, she said, "Your yard is impeccable. It must take a lot of your time."

He turned to the yard. "I have someone who comes around from time to time."

"And that big fire pit. Nice for these cool nights. It would really look nice with a stone half-wall for sitting."

"I sit up here," he said, offering a seat.

"A little weather stain and a light sanding would clean up those chair runners nicely. I haven't sat in a big rocker like this since I was a little girl," she said, admiring the quaint property.

Mr. Mortimer assessed the woman who hadn't stopped smiling since she'd arrived, despite her periodic attempts to elicit comment or confession.

"You're a very observant woman, Detective. I can't tell if you're looking to move in or sell my home."

She gushed. "Sometimes I get a little fixated. My husband and I recently moved to the area. I can't say that I loved the homes we saw. But this. This reminds me of some of the homes around the

Detroit suburbs, but so much more well-maintained. And what a lovely yard to raise children."

"Let's get that water for you, and a glass for me. I'd planned to show you more inside, anyway. It's much less inspiring. Still, I'm quite hospitable to people with fixations." Mr. Mortimer escorted his guest toward the back of the wrap. There was yet another door. "What brought you here to this area?"

"New job."

"There isn't much crime in Skokie. I can't imagine a detective leaving Detroit. Unless she had nothing to detect?"

Her smile broke. "Touché."

Mr. Mortimer tilted his head, begging for more with a tight-lipped grin.

"My husband travels and can work anywhere. Skokie, it is. But to answer you, big city means big crime. My bosses felt I always tried to tie unsolved murders and disappearances to serial killers." She shrugged. "I just follow the data, but police departments like easy, solvable cases. I thought a place like Skokie might make things less complex. But here I am, wrapped up in another."

He raised his eyebrows over his glasses. "And you suspect a serial killer handled the boy and his father?"

"Not at all. I used to do serial killer research in partnership with Florida Gulf Coast University. They have a massive database. Pet project for me. Ironically, once my husband and I moved here, this part of the Chicago area showed in the Radford database as a white space where nothing happens."

"That's good to hear. Safe."

"Or maybe too good. Anyway. Just a hobby and a hunch. Sometimes when a serial killer gets sloppy or wants to get caught, they kill in their own areas. This could be the area that was saved for last, or just sanctuary."

He nodded in understanding as they stopped at the door. "Or...tie up loose ends before they move away. I can make you some lemonade if you prefer. Sweet tea, if you don't mind it from a bottle."

"Water is fine."

"Water, it is." His grin turned toothy.

"You'll appreciate the interesting layout. The house was a series of additions and partitioning. It had been an old crematorium before anyone now living in the area could remember. A series of parlors. A large furnace and hand crank bone crusher in the basement serviced by a hand-pull elevator in the garage. It can get confusing. Even for me in my old age. A solver of puzzles will love it."

Mr. Mortimer opened the glass storm door and pushed the wooden one behind it to reveal a sparse but inviting interior that indeed showed some structural obsolescence with what appeared to be rooms adjoined to connected rooms.

"Wow, I see what you mean." She took a step closer to the entry.

As he held open the entry, he extended his long arm outward, guiding her inside. "Yes, we can talk better in here," he coaxed as she stepped past him.

Detective Jefferson's face soured at a faint odor. She sniffed at the air, trying to catch the scent. She traced the putrid aroma, a whiff of revulsive decay. It was his breath. Jefferson wanted to gag from the horrific stench. From the glass reflection, she caught Mr. Mortimer looking behind himself and scanning his view to the street. Something triggered an instant flashback warning in Jefferson from her first years as a detective. Her breath froze in the middle of her chest, and her fingers rolled inward to a clench of despair. Her jaw quivered as she took another unwilling step inward with legs that weakened in protest. He continued to guide her forward to the inside. Her shoulders and elbows tensed to her sides as panic crashed her system in foreboding peril, and from her throat to her face, her skin burned with pinprick tingles that surged to her ears. Her breath hadn't returned. She fought high in her chest to pull air. Anxiety swirled about her, stealing her wits and flushing her with confusion, nausea, and disassociation.

The man gripped her upper arm. "Careful, he warned. "There

WHISPERS OF A GYPSY

is a bit of a step as you walk in. I find myself tripping often. Growing habit."

Detective Jefferson heard his muffled words as her own thoughts of the past swirled in her mind. His spoken voice sounded like it was inside her head. Like a memory. Oh, that memory she tried each day to forget. His grasp grew tighter. She fought to snap her body out of the shock and respond to her mind, which was screaming, "RUN!", but could only shuffle forward against her will. Something was pulling at her fear. Probing for a way in.

The strength of the man lifting her into the house caused greater concern. She was wrong. He was strong. Very strong. *Like him.* Possibly overpowering. *Like him.* It was no longer the grip of a feeble old man who'd just fallen and scraped himself on the side-walk. *The bleeding. It was bad. I hadn't imagined it. Short of a red smear when he was on the porch and wiped his chin, there was no cut. They said he was the killer. He killed them. Now he's trying to kill me. Oh, my God, I'm going to die. My kids will never know. They tried to warn me. I'm going to pass out. I think I'm going to pass out. I can't go through this again. No. You can't have it.*

Her mind raced, and she heeded to a subconscious fight-or-flight reflex. Her mind fought. Her body fought. It was too strong. In the distance came another voice. Her head cooled. It calmed her with calm feelings, subtle sensations, smooth move-ment, and soft rhythms. She heard the small voice of another whisper in her head. A boy?

It's okay. He won't. Hurt you.

Detective Jefferson snapped her arms up to the doorframe and locked them to stop. She swiveled her head while reaching into her covered shoulder holster.

"Dwight?" she gasped.

Mr. Mortimer released his grip.

Dwight Skinner stepped up to the old man and gave him a chastising swat. "I don't like. When you wear that. Color. Black. Blech. Mean."

Detective Jefferson's mobile device rang. She snatched it. "Hi, Momma. I'm here in Skokie at a man named Mortimer Eiserman's house, with a boy named Dwight Skinner. Is everything okay?"

As her mother spoke, Detective Jefferson backed up out of the door frame and took the deepest breath of her life. Her emotions built up and were ready to burst, but she had to let someone know where she was, and whom she was with. She'd learned that.

"Momma, I'm just running a minute late. Can I call you right back from the car? Okay. Love you, Momma. Yes, I do. Well, I'm telling you I love you today, and I appreciate you. All right. Call you in a few. Bye." She paced around in a quick circle, exhaling.

"Detective, are you alright?" Mr. Mortimer asked, with genuine concern. He held Dwight's hand in his. "I didn't mean to cause you alarm."

She shook her head, then nodded yes. Finally, as she slowed and sized up the old man and young boy in his snorkeling gear, both standing at a Pippi Longstocking-looking house, she shuddered and realized a trigger from the past must have set her off.

"Dwight, does your mother know you're here?"

"Yes, she told. Me to. Come here. Detective."

"Mmmm, no, baby, I don't think so. I think maybe you need to come with me back to your house." She extended her hand toward the child in the international sign language of mothers that said, *We're going now.* "Thank you, sir, but I'll have to come back another time."

"The boy can stay," Mr. Mortimer challenged back. "He's no bother at all."

Detective Jefferson's adrenaline was still in overdrive. She grabbed Dwight's hand and shuttled him down the steps. "I don't think so. Baby, I'll get you back home to your momma."

"It's okay," Esther said, stepping into view from the front of the porch. "I told him to come. I need to take care of my *shomeret* duties until burial." She sighed. "Would that be okay? Mr. Mortimer? Eiserman?"

Dwight scampered back up the steps, looked up at the tall old man, and reached out for his hand. "I'm going to play. With Mr. Monster. C'mon. Let's play. *It's okay,*" he whispered to the detective.

Detective Jefferson raced to her car, not turning back.

Chapter Twenty-Eight

Dwight climbed onto the large porch chair. "Can I rock?"

"We both can," Mr. Mortimer said, with a grin. "I like to make the boards creak." Mortimer pushed with his feet to lean way back. He lifted his legs, and the chair pitched forward and back, unleashing a long, loud creak and a hearty laugh from Dwight.

Mr. Mortimer beckoned Esther to join them. "Mrs. Skinner, you've had a horrible day. If you care to return home, I can keep an eye on the boy. If you prefer to close your eyes in my house, there's a worn leather sofa as effective as the Sandman himself. Let the officials do their duties. You don't need to be there. Perhaps a small glass of bourbon and some rest would do you good."

Esther seemed to contemplate the offer.

"Please make yourself at home. The boy and I will find something to do outside."

Esther held herself and shook her head. "I have to go back. I can't leave them. It's *my* duty."

Mr. Mortimer tilted his glasses down, raising an eyebrow yet again. "Your husband was not a Jew, Mrs. Skinner. You're not a real Jew. You choose to live under the laws. For safety? You are not safe. There is an investigation. I regret that they may remove the bodies if they haven't already. Now is the time to be with family. If you wish to return home for something your husband and son once owned, we can burn it at the fire. Today, your family is here. The people of your father's father."

"I can't. I have something to do." Esther turned away from the house and broke into a run.

Dwight rocked back and forth in futility, like a turtle on its back. His snorkel flowed with the motion.

Mortimer sat in his chair and reached across to give Dwight a good pull and push. He let fly, and the boy produced his own loud creaks. The laughs continued until Dwight's increasing momentum flung him to the floor.

Mr. Mortimer lifted the young boy up and set him on his lap. The old man wiped a solitary tear that dripped down the boy's cheek as he rocked. "Just a small fall, no need for a cry," he consoled him as he wrapped his long arms around Dwight.

"Do you. Cry?" the boy asked.

"Never anymore."

Dwight turned and touched Mr. Mortimer's chin. "Not even. When. You hurt?"

"I don't get hurt."

"That's a. Hurt." Dwight pushed on the fading chin scab.

"It goes away."

"Where do. You hurt. That doesn't. Go away?" Dwight asked.

"Sometimes here." Mr. Mortimer pointed to his breast, his flesh wound healed but a lifetime of heartfelt pains still open and festering. "Never here," he said of his arms and legs.

Dwight pulled back. He hammered down on Mr. Mortimer's arm, resting across the chair, and looked up for a reaction. "Never?"

Nothing.

"That wasn't very nice," Mr. Mortimer scolded. "It felt hateful. It hurt me here." Mr. Mortimer pointed to his arm. "And here." He moved his finger to his chest once more.

The tears started again from Dwight. "I'm sorry. I hit you. Are you. Mad?"

"I could never be mad at you, Dwight. I was friends with your grandfather and loved him very much when he was of pure heart. So much that I could eat his belly."

"You ate his. Belly?"

"It's a phrase of my people. Your people. I didn't eat it." He rubbed the boy's head. "And we're friends, right?"

"Best friends." Dwight wrapped his arms around Mr. Mortimer in a tight embrace.

"We're like brothers, right?"

Dwight released his arms and pulled back. He gave a serious nod. "I miss. My brother. He was. My best. Friend."

"I know you loved him, too. Even though he was naughty to you."

"I'd marry. Him," Dwight said resolutely, as if there could be no doubt in the obvious. He pointed a finger at Mr. Mortimer's chest. "I'd marry. You."

Mr. Mortimer extended a finger under his glasses. His finger was wet when he pulled it back out. "Do you know what blood brothers are?"

"Vampires." Dwight laughed. "Argh," he said, lunging forward and biting the air.

"No, blood brothers cut their hands and shake on it."

"I don't want. To get cut."

"It's a small cut."

"Will it. Hurt?"

"Not if you don't look."

"Then we shake. Hands. And we are. Brothers. For life?"

"I'll give you some of my blood, and you give me some of yours. It's a trade."

"My mom. Won't want me. To take blood. Out. Can I. Just have. Some of. Yours?"

"Let me show you something."

Mr. Mortimer poured bourbon whiskey into two glasses.

From one, he poured the liquid to the top. "What happens if I pour more?"

"It spills. And makes a. Mess. And mom. Yells."

"Exactly. So, if I take a little out," he sips, "I can pour more in."

"If I gave. You. My blood. And you had yours. Full. It would. Come out of. My eyes. And mouth. And explode. And get on. All the houses." Dwight smiled.

Mortimer laughed. "It could."

"So, we need. To just. Trade some?"

"And then you would have my powers, too. Like a dynamic duo, for real." Mr. Mortimer sloughed his chin scab. It fell to the porch floor. The wound was healed.

"Wow. And you. Have. My. Super. Powers. Do we use. A knife. Or does a shark. Bite. Us?"

"I have a little something." Mr. Mortimer drew from under his jacket an old recycled Churi peg knife. He pressed the blade into his palm and slid it across, unzipping the red life from under his skin. "Now you?"

"Okay," Dwight said, still unsure. He bit his lip before asking, "Will you. Bring. My body. To. My mom?"

"What?"

"If it doesn't. Work. So, I can. Be buried. Near my. Brother."

"You think you will die from the cut?"

Dwight bobbed his head, affirming.

"Then why did you agree?"

"So, you. Stay. My friend."

Mr. Mortimer was speechless. After a moment, he said, "Dwight, look," and held open his hand. The stain remained, but the opening was sealed. Mr. Mortimer scissored his fingers across the healed wound, showing no more bleeding.

"Super. Powers. I want super powers. I want. To fly."

"I can give this to you, too. To strengthen you. Heal your brain and your body. Just like we can talk to each other without our mouths."

"Like I do. With my mom. When she. Whispers."

"Your mother knows the whisper?"

Detective Jefferson navigated the Skokie police station
hallways to her small, nondescript office.

"Momma, I just needed to buy some time. Yes, I'm okay. I just
got a little creeped out, is all, with an investigation I'm working
on. I'll be by to get the kids in a couple hours. And I'll bring
dinner." She paused. "Roger's coming home, so he'll be there in
the next hour or so. Yes, I love you, too."

Detective Jefferson stretched her back as the computer screen
booted up. Her nerves were still firing.

She typed the name "Mortimer Eiserman" into the National
Crime Information Center's database. As the screen loaded, she
shifted to another monitor and searched the Henry Wallace Police
Crime Database. From the third screen, she opened the Kologik
Public Safety Platform with integrated Thomson Reuters search
capability. Upon the last keystroke, she sat back, waiting for the
first scan to populate with what she deemed a material hit.

Nothing. At least nothing out of the ordinary. Old guy
towing the line.

She exhaled.

Detective Jefferson cleared the entries and pulled up Google.
She typed the same. Nothing. She added "immigration" to his
name in the search, hoping to find some records from a family
database and national record entries.

Nothing.

She typed "Holocaust Survivors." Google showed the Database of Holocaust Survivors and Victim Names, which she also
selected, then input the name.

Nothing.

"Damn." She leaned back, disappointed but not surprised.

She typed the address of Mr. Mortimer in the county tax

assessor's database. "North Shore Crematorium? How long have you lived there?"

Shrugging, she typed "Esther Skinner" in public records.

"Holy crap."

"Detective." The booming voice of her chief gave Detective Jefferson a jump.

"Sir?"

"I need you on another case. M.E. is ruling the Skinner case a murder-suicide."

"Chief, I think there's-"

"Detective, if there was something important you needed to share with me, I probably would have seen you in my office before I came to you. So hold that thought." He started with a finger point. "I went out on a limb bringing you in. Your candidacy helped us diversify, and we helped you when a lot of departments would have been reluctant with your serial killer fantasies."

"If you read my file, that fantasy was a suspect under my department's investigation radar, who about killed me. Not my fault. And if that stupid chief would have-"

He held up a hand. "Stop. Just stop. I see where you may have had some problems in the past, given the feedback I've gotten from Moshe. I assigned you to this case for you to learn from him. Learn about these people. Understand community policing in a different community."

"I've been doing that."

"Did you curse at a rabbi and physically prevent him from doing what this department and community pay him to do?"

"I don't think he's telling us all he knows."

The chief rolled his eyes. "And how long have you known him, versus the decade I have?"

Detective Jefferson's tongue toyed with her teeth, and she evaluated her next words and whether she valued her job. "What if we had a serial killer in our midst?"

The chief whistled. "That's it. Go home. Come back

tomorrow if you can work for me, and not for yourself. That's how I run my shop. I told them this was a mistake."

"This?" She circled her face with her hand. "Or me. I'm not a 'this.'"

"Goodnight, Detective. Turn off your computer. Let's go."

"Sir, I-"

"Let's go. We'll call you when we have a serial killer case. Until then, everything's good in Skokie, except for punks and a dad who whacked himself and his kid to get back at his wife. If you can't see that, you need to open your eyes to this town."

Detective Jefferson closed out of her databases and screens. She committed to memory the news headline on her screen.

Woman Dies in Accident, Injured Sister Delivers Baby.

Chapter Twenty-Nine

Sitting up in bed, kids asleep and husband trying to catch some shut-eye, Detective Jefferson tilted her readers further down her nose, squinting to see the print. She read aloud in a fast, robotic murmur, joining all the words into a long, drawn-out drone that was beyond annoying to Rodger, who had a 5 o'clock wake-up call for an early morning meeting.

"This lady, never married and worked with Esther's husband, the two sisters are in a car accident, which Mrs. Skinner said, but her sister had a child on the scene, sister dies in the accident, other sister survives. That's the other kid."

She lifted her head, gobsmacked.

Groaning like a child forced to eat spinach, her husband said, "You do know I'm not listening and have no idea what you're even talking about."

"It wasn't hers," she said aloud to herself. "Don't worry, I'm not talking to you. It was the dad and sister's. Makes you wonder why no women are on death row but there are so many unsolved murders?"

Her bedmate flopped over like a breaching whale and folded the pillow over his head in frustration.

"Sorry, but since you're still awake, real quick help me

through this," she said, not moving her head from the captivating research glowing blue across her glasses. "Don't give me any attitude either. You've been gone all week and are back out tomorrow. I've had quite a day, too. Met a guy who'd been tested on by Nazis. Holocaust survivor. Scared the crap out of me. Thought I was going to die, again. Like, really. Looked up the wife's family history and their business. It all links to some crazy stuff. Listen to this."

"Do I have a choice? Wait? Did he attack you?"

"No," she said. "I mean, you don't really have a choice, and he didn't attack me, but I thought he might. My head went back to Ron Littig."

"That guy who tried to kill you. What did this guy do?"

"He didn't do anything. I need to do some research on contemporary eugenics."

"I'm not doing this." He buried himself back in the covers. From under the pillow, he relented and asked, "Is that L. Ron Hubbard?"

"Don't be stupid. I'm serious." She tugged at his pillow. "I'm looking at the family of this murder suicide. And then there's the guy from the Holocaust. It looks like because of what happened in concentration camps, there's this business and link to gene therapies and research. It's really interesting. Has a lot of impacts for kids, too. C'mon. Read with me."

"Fine. You want a designer baby?"

"No, but yeah, that's kind of it. Wait. How do you know about this?"

"I read it on the plane. Contrary to your belief that I'm sleeping or watching downloaded shows."

"Hmm...color me impressed. Oh, that's another thing I need to tell you about. Don't let me forget. Anyway, this thing is called a CRISPR-Cas-nine that can edit DNA by removing or changing genes for a healthy population."

Rodger flopped over again. "Doesn't seem like a bad thing if it can get rid of crazy people. Baby, turn out the lights."

"Just a few more minutes." The detective rubbed her husband's shoulder. "Then I'll give you some lovin'."

He sat up. "What are we looking at?"

She side-eyed him with a smirk. "Embryo selection could be done without consent."

"That's in the future, and we're not having more kids."

"Stop. This has been going on since the Nazis," she said. "Everyone seems so focused on concentration camps, they never looked into the medical experience and what they call 'medicalized killing.' These doctors justified it."

"Their wives didn't give them a choice."

"Oh, my God. Did you just say that?" She swatted him.

"Okay, we're doing this, I see." He put on his glasses and turned to what she was reading. "This is work, right? I'm not doing this because you started with the sniffles on WebMD and now can't get out of your rabbit hole."

She pointed to a page. "Aspirin. Can you believe it?"

"Lord, have mercy. Catch me up."

She smiled. "I knew you'd find this interesting. This Zyclon B they used in gas chambers came from the company IG Farben. That's where Bayer, the company for aspirin, came from. Monsanto."

"That's Round-Up. Weedkiller. Just saw there's a cancer lawsuit."

She said nothing in response and continued reading to herself with the same rapid-fire murmur.

Roger reached across himself to the nightstand, where he grabbed his iPhone and television remote. He turned on the television and channel-hopped until he found something.

She turned. "I thought you were helping me?"

"I am."

"Not if you're watching television."

"You're reading to yourself."

She pointed to her laptop screen. "Monsanto was genetically altering seeds, while sister companies were genetically altering animals. Their research was tied to a university. The University of Strasbourg in partnership with Joseph Mengele. They made shots for viruses." She looked over to her husband.

He was beaming while watching his show.

"This that show where you keep sayin', 'I'm your Huckleberry?'"

"No. That's *Tombstone*. This is *Silverado*."

She watched the movie intently for a moment. "That's Danny Glover."

"Yeah. He's good."

"You watched this last week."

He pointed to the television like a child. "I know, but it's on again."

She held out her hand for the remote control. "Rodger Ainsley Jefferson."

He turned off the television. "What do you need me to do?"

"Google 'University of Strasbourg' and 'genetics.'"

He thumbed the device and said, "Institute of Genetics and Molecular and Cellular Biology."

"Ugh. I don't need another rabbit hole." She turned back to her own screen.

Roger kept reading. After a couple minutes, he said, "They do cool stuff."

Not paying much attention, she soon asked, "Like?"

"Stem cells, neurogenetics. They got a big grant for DNA testing."

"Like those ancestor tests."

He said nothing, but his brow caved.

"Like where you spit in the tube?"

Still nothing. His mouth moved like he'd tasted something foul.

"It's no help if you keep it a secret."

He showed her the phone screen. "Is this what you wanted to see?"

Her face fell. "I feel sick."

"That's only the first one. Look at this." His finger scrolled down.

"Wuhan Institute of Virology."

He rolled over and turned out the nightstand light.

"I'm not done reading," she said and turned on her overhead reading light.

"Yes, you are." He reached over to turn off her light.

Detective Jefferson slapped at his hand. "Can you imagine if all this COVID and monkeypox and other lab modified viruses were used to target specific genetics to weed out the weak or...or races?"

"Stop," he protested. "I'm not reading stuff like that before I go to bed."

"Afraid you'll have nightmares?"

"Afraid of what if it's true." Rodger crossed his arms and closed his eyes.

"Which part?"

"What part would you want to be true, Detective Jefferson? Imagine millions of people giving their DNA to a lab that can make a guess on what anyone else from a race could have. Then come up with a way to wipe out entire people they don't want. Blacks, Mexicans, Jews, Arabs, you name it. Poor folks. Tell you what, minorities better be thinking of that."

"Mr. Mortimer. Eiserman. Oh, my word."

"Who?" Rodger opened his eyes.

"One last thing, and I'll stop." She started typing.

"Stace. Where's your head going now?"

"Looking for dead Nazi scientists."

"Well, they won't be a problem." He flipped over to his opposite side, pulling a blanket over his head.

"Here's one. Operation Paperclip. Walter Schreiber, yadda, yadda, Nazi bioweapon general. Okay. Specialty, viral and bacteriological warfare. That's a serious truth bomb."

He sighed and flipped the covers back down. "I'll go make some coffee. Need to go back to Detroit. It wasn't good, but at least I could sleep. Forget the Nazis. If you read down the grants to that university, there are a bunch of U.S. locations. I already read that. A New York School of Science and Technology, a Brooklyn-Queens Facility." He chuckled. "Man, they probably made *Captain America* here. Got any big green guys running around with supernatural strength?"

Detective Jefferson kept her focus.

Her husband continued. "There's a lab in Illinois. Let me click on this. SSR Locations. Click this, too. Bam. The Strategic Science Research Great Lakes Facility. About ten or fifteen miles from here in Northfield, just off the expressway. Right in your back yard."

"Northfield. Within the Radford circle."

"Aw jeez. Here we go with your serial killer conspiracies."

"Killed. The husband, father-in-law, and sister all worked there."

"Who's?"

"Esther Skinner. And her son has a genetic disorder."

Chapter Thirty

T he prospect of Esther being able to whisper like her ancestors wasn't altogether surprising to Mr. Mortimer, especially given the nature of their auspices being a conservative Jewish family. Yitzhak Skinner had spoken highly of his daughter-in-law, but other details aside from her being Saul's granddaughter remained inconsequential.

Still, it surprised Mr. Mortimer when Esther returned nearly an hour later to his home with her arms full.

"I hope the offer still stands," she said, stepping up the porch stairs. "The synagogue sent some volunteers to perform *shemira*. They'll stay all night, chatting away and reciting from Psalms."

Mr. Mortimer raised a finger to his lips. "He just fell asleep after we started the fire and danced." Dwight was covered in a small blanket and cuddled up in the rocking chair.

"Oh, no. I'm so sorry. I can take him back home. I didn't mean to be a burden. Wait, did you say you were dancing?"

"Who doesn't enjoy dancing around a fire? Please sit. Did you gather some items for a traditional send-off?"

Esther looked down at the bundle in her arms. "I...I didn't mean to. I mean, I wasn't going to come back for a while. The investigators and everyone are all gone. The house doesn't feel the same. It's so surreal." Esther cried. "I just sat on the couch, poured a glass of wine, and realized I didn't want to be there." She sniffled and gave a nervous laugh. "So, I brought it here with my blanket and a little food for you and Dwight, and I grabbed a couple items like you suggested. I don't have anywhere else to go."

Dwight stirred in Mr. Mortimer's lap.

Esther smiled, but it looked forced. "I'm confused. I thought you didn't like children?"

Mr. Mortimer continued rocking the sleeping boy. "I like this one. I like the ones before they become part of the world. They become like their parents. They learn to hate. I always wanted a son. I never wanted them to change. To be part of the problem."

Esther set the bottle down on the table with a couple glasses. She sat in the rocker, put the memory items at her feet, and spread the blanket across her. As she fidgeted to make appropriate time before diving straight into the bottle, she replied, "I'm sorry I don't know this, but were you ever...I mean, was there anyone?"

Mr. Mortimer shook his head. "It wasn't meant to be. There was always war. Barriers. Then it was taken from me."

"Yitzhak never spoke of the war. He mentioned a Gypsy saved him. I'm guessing that was you."

Mr. Mortimer nodded.

"Was your family there? With you? In the camps?"

"No. My father was killed in the Great War. I was a soldier, too. Poland. When the Nazis came, I was among those conscripted to wipe out slums. Ethnic enclaves. They threatened to kill my family. I did as I was ordered. Killed. Until we were ordered to wipe out the countryside where my mother and sisters lived. I disobeyed the orders and resisted. After driving me to deeds inconceivable to my character. From victim to criminal. The Germans shot me. I should have died."

"Oh, God."

"They shot little Itzhak to provoke me. Yitzhak. Your father-in-law's name before we were liberated. He should have died, too. We would have, perhaps, been better if we'd died." Mr. Mortimer stared into the fire. "This boy helps me forget what I see around me."

"Well, I agree. This guy is the most amazing boy, but he's a handful, as I'm sure you can tell."

"Boys will be boys. They are difficult when they resist their environment. They are difficult when they enthusiastically embrace their environment. This one's heart resists his surroundings. Compassion, and the unconditionality of it, are his true gift. I envy him."

"That's rather...deep."

"What is his genetic affliction?"

"Excuse me?"

"I may not know the right way to speak without offending, but part of his charm and loving self has to do with his simple state. If you would share, I'd like to know what it is."

"He was born with it. Abnormal cell division. Affects his appearance, learning, development. Although, he's always been very high functioning. Even at a young age, it was difficult to tell. But we were in a car accident. My sister died. Dwight was injured badly. There was some brain damage. That's what also causes his speech patterns. The rest is just Dwight."

"Thank you. That is helpful."

"That's also when he started seeing and relating to everything with colors," Esther added.

"The accident?"

Esther unscrewed the wine top. "Can I offer you a glass? The wine is quite good. They say screw caps are better."

"Please." Mr. Mortimer stared off into the fire and accepted the glass. As Esther drank, he whispered, "Te bisterdon tumor anava."

She coughed.

"You can hear my whispers in the mind, but you don't know what it means?" Mr. Mortimer laughed. "I think in his heart, Yitzhak always wanted to be a Jew."

Esther wiped the spilled wine from her chin with the blanket. She said nothing.

"I toasted their names would never be forgotten. At this point, you can toss their personal items into the fire. When they are gone in the flames, you and I can talk about why you are here, and you can tell me where Yitzhak Skinner left my notebooks. I know, in truth, you despise being in my presence."

Esther stood and looked behind her to the dark streets. She returned her focus to the fire and collected a toy of Aaron's and shirt of David's.

Mr. Mortimer gathered Dwight's gangly legs and propped him gently in the chair before following Esther to the fire. Upon taking a deep drink of the red wine, he added, "It's ironic about the Gypsy persecution and the Romani tongue. They tried to eliminate us, and yet we were the true Aryans. A rather inconvenient misunderstanding of history while they treated us worse than the *Juden*. I believe Hitler knew this. His allure to the mysticism. To our ties to a veritable goddess, Kali, in India. The supernatural, which for us is natural. Gypsy magic is in understanding people. It is amazing with all the torture, beatings, and interrogation, *they never learned of the whispers.* Therefore, I need the book with the names. The names of my people they experimented on. The research I want destroyed. There are far more powers the few of us with direct lineage can summon. Those of us who are not just Gypsies or Romani but rather belong to the Punjab Kala mountain priests. We come from both darkness and time. From Kali, mother nature, thus our ties to all that is around us." *Om Kring Kalikaye Namah.*

Esther cringed as he entered her mind for the moment. She tossed the shirt and toy into the fire like they were trash. "Get out of my head. Stop this voodoo and fairy tale nonsense."

"Do you know why our people burn the possessions of the dead?" Mr. Mortimer asked.

"They are *your* people. Not *my* people."

"You are *my* people, Esther. Your family line. The boy is *my* people. Your husband and son, as much as I did not care for them, were also *my* people. My blood."

"They're dead. You don't deserve to speak of them," she warned him.

"I have to speak of them," he contested. "The dead can come back. When we burn their possessions, we ask for their forgiveness and settle our debts. Otherwise, the dead can be a threat to the living."

"I'll never ask for my husband's forgiveness. What he did to my son and me. How he treated Aaron and turned him against Dwight. They were brothers, for God's sake."

Mr. Mortimer kicked at the fire. "Aaron was your sister's son, wasn't he? Perhaps even your husband's child? David Skinner was a dirty *rahat* like his mistress's boy at an even younger age. The boy was your blood. You had responsibility for his behavior."

"I know what you are." She turned to Mr. Mortimer. The fire's glow showed a sternness on her face. "I know what you did to my husband and sister's son."

"Of course you do. I'm sure they told you. But the question is, what did *you* and *Dwight* do to them once I left?"

A voice spoke just behind the edge of the firelight. "Don't answer that, Ms. Skinner."

In rapid succession, three gunshots popped in the otherwise silent night.

Mr. Mortimer fell into the fire, sending sparks and embers high in his flame-fanning wake. His body lay lifeless as his clothing combusted to a growing inferno that consumed his form.

Esther Skinner screamed.

Behind her cry of terror came the sound of a metal sliding door, revving of an engine, and the screech of tires clawing for purchase on asphalt.

As silence returned to the night, a small, fading voice whispered from the van, "Monster?"

Chapter Thirty-One

Esther's screaming persisted for what seemed to be an endless capacity of breath and terror.

"They weren't supposed to take him. That wasn't the deal. Oh, my God, that wasn't the deal." She repeated the self-chastisement over and over as Mr. Mortimer lay burning before her.

As Dwight traveled farther away, emergency response vehicles drew closer. Within minutes, Mr. Mortimer's pristine property was filled with red and blue strobes and people dashing about with their own white lights.

Sparks and embers rose to the sky as two police officers dragged Mr. Mortimer's charred corpse from the hot coals and flames. They dropped a large blanket to extinguish the fire.

"That dude's a dead burnt marshmallow," the officer said to his peer.

"Smell's horrible," the other responded.

"We should have kept him on longer. He'd at least be easier to stick in a body bag."

"Let's let him cool off a bit. We can wait in the bus. I gotta show you this video I got last week on the DL of an accident scene."

. . .

E sther's hands shook and breaths were high and rapid while the officers questioned her. Her head pounded.

"Oh, God, they have my boy. They took my boy."

Officer Rodriguez was back on the scene. "Ma'am, we're going to do everything we can. Please, we need more information."

"Get me Detective Jefferson. She'll know what to do. Can you call her? I can get you the number at my home. It's just down the street."

"Ma'am, we can call Detective Jefferson. Is there anyone else you need us to call? Your husband? Oh, geez. Sorry. Maybe a friend."

She shook her head. "There's no one. I don't have. . ."

"Okay, ma'am, please. Just try to calm down." Rodriguez called out to another officer walking up the drive, "Get Detective Jefferson out here. Let's get this woman inside."

The approaching officer, Miller, put his hands on his hips, taking in the scene. "Man, I always wanted to go inside this old house. I heard they used to burn people right in the basement."

E sther had made a tragic mistake. She would have been better off going to Rabbi Dratch. Instead, she made the call both her grandfather and father-in-law said to use only in an emergency if she had something to barter. All these things raced in her panicking mind, which had been a flurry of open-ended questions since the shooting.

As she was escorted up the porch steps and into the home, she looked back at the covered heap near the fire, wondering if she'd just informed on the only person — or thing — that could get her son back.

Once a Kapo, always a Kapo.

Chapter Thirty-Two

Officer Miller waved his flashlight across the walls. "Where are the lights in this place?"

Officer Rodriguez flipped a switch, to no avail. "Maybe there's a fuse box we can pop."

Miller's light strobed from floor to ceiling. "Unless they turned off the power from ComEd. There's hardly any furniture in here."

"Ma'am, do you know who lives here?" Rodriguez asked. "Was it the person you said was shot in the yard?"

Esther was leaning back on the kitchen counter in a catatonic state. She was wrapped in a blanket with her hands curled around the edges and lifted to her chin. She didn't reply.

"Ma'am?" Rodriguez echoed. "Do you know who lives here?"

"Mr. Eiserman," she replied. "He was the man in the yard."

Miller shone his light on Esther. "Is he moving in or out? Do you know if lights work?"

She shook her head.

"No, there are no lights, or no, you don't know?" Miller pressed.

She shrugged and slipped out of her catatonic state. "He seems to come and go. Sometimes we may not see him out for walks for weeks or months at a time. I assume he has people who take care of the house. I heard my father-in-law say something to my husband. I didn't know it was about him at the time. He may have friends who live up north, near the Wisconsin border."

"I'm going to look around," Miller said. "Place is creepy."

～

Detective Jefferson was at the scene within minutes. She passed the emergency techs chatting in their ambulance. Clearly no rush to the hospital. The fire pit was smoldering. A red rescue blanket lay unfolded on the ground. She headed toward the moving lights near the back of the house through the door that had raised her panic. Why the EMTs were just sitting around in their truck while a body was presumably in the back was anyone's guess.

Meanwhile, Officer Miller scouted each room with his colleague, flipping light switches as they passed. "This place is a friggin' maze of rooms. Each one leads to another room leading to a new room."

"My guess is, they did medical examinations in some of these and probably had cold storage or labs attached," Rodriguez shared. "I wouldn't be surprised if they just dry-walled over the old brick framing."

Miller touched the walls. "How do you even know all this? This place has been around for decades."

"My dad grew up down the street. Building was owned by the state and then abandoned until it got picked up years later. My dad used to throw rocks at the windows."

"Explains why you're a cop, then, coming from such a law-abiding family."

Rodriguez laughed. "My dad's a lawyer."

"Figures."

"So far, I've seen one sofa with a side table. No television.

No chairs. Nothing. Should we check out upstairs?" Rodriguez cast his light up to the top flight. A dark hallway appeared expansive.

Miller put the light on his own face. "I want to see where they cooked the bodies. Want to come? One of these doorways has to lead to a basement."

The two men wound around yet another odd room attachment and found themselves by the front door, which was open.

Rodriguez stopped. "Do you remember this door being open when we got here?"

Miller walked toward it. "You mean you were looking at anything besides a woman screaming and a body bonfire?"

"Facts."

M r. Mortimer passed from room to room in the shadows until he reached a door to the lower level. He descended the stairs as lights flickered in the hallways. He held the rails tight along both sides of the wall to steady his failing body, wheezing with each step.

In the kitchen, Detective Jefferson stood patiently as Esther Skinner continued a circuitous monologue of how she'd contacted a man who took over her father-in-law's lab and was willing to help her son. Her son had been taken, but she was unsure of who actually took him.

"Mrs. Skinner," Detective Jefferson chimed in on a hunch, "what kind of help was this person going to give your son, and do you have a name and address for us?"

"I just had a number. The person knew my grandfather from years ago."

"That helps. And Mrs. Skinner, did that man have any business dealings with your father-in-law or the research he was involved with?"

"I'm not sure."

Detective Jefferson grew impatient, knowing she could be

getting more half-truths. "You're not sure, but you knew *specifically* this person could help your son. And what was that help?"

Esther said nothing for a moment. "Medical."

"Medical. And did this medical have anything to do with cell therapies? Maybe a research lab northeast of town?"

As a wave of panic washed over Esther, she heard a whisper. *Say nothing. Sa te fut. You gadji curva Kapo. Get these police out of my house. I'll come to your home tonight if you wish to save your son from being torn apart like a lab rat. This is why Yitzhak refused to help him.*

"Detective, I have to get to my home." Esther started for the door.

"Mrs. Skinner, I'll go with you, but-"

"No. No, I'm sorry I troubled you to come."

"They would have had me or someone else out here, anyway. It's a crime scene, and I still don't know what happened."

"He's dead and burned. My son is gone, and my husband and son are dead in my living room, where I'm supposed to be sitting with them. Because *that* is my duty."

Detective Jefferson stepped from the kitchen to what, in the darkness, looked like another room. "Let me check with the other officers." She heard the back door shut. "Damn."

Esther raced back home, seeking refuge in the darkness and shadows. Hands trembling, she poured herself a glass of wine and sat at the kitchen table, waiting and walking back in her mind to the lies she'd told that evening. She remembered the call she'd made earlier. Mr. Mortimer was right, although she couldn't translate all that he whispered in his native tongue, one word seared her core being — Kapo. Like the individuals chosen in the labor camps by the SS guards, it was attributed to selling out for privilege. She did exactly that to the very same people who'd imprisoned her people both in bloodline and association. Whether she was a Jew or Roma, she gave up another of her kind for personal gain.

Esther downed the wine, poured another, rested her face in

her palms, and cried.

A blistered, charred, and swollen hand lowered to her shoulder. "I need food in order to save your child."

Esther jumped from her chair. "How did you get in here? How are you not dead?" She gagged at the sight and smell of charred flesh and pervasive rot that emanated from Mr. Mortimer's mouth. His body was blackened, scorched flesh curled from muscle and bone, and patches of raw meat bled.

Esther dashed to the sink and vomited.

Ignoring the question, Mr. Mortimer repeated, "I need to eat if you want to save your child. I need it immediately."

She pointed to the food haphazardly placed about the kitchen by the women from the community who'd learned of her husband and son's passing. There were bagels on the counter. Two platters. Boiled eggs on the table, in the refrigerator, and by the stove. Rugelach was by the lentils.

"That won't do."

The fire had destroyed Mr. Mortimer's facial skin and underlying tissue. His head was a cornucopia of blacks, browns, and yellow. Smoked muscle and cheekbones peeked through the burnt open wounds. His black eyes bore into hers. From his mouth of swollen and broken lips, his yellowed teeth now appeared lighter.

He said, "I need strength. I need...to replace. It requires stem cell extraction. Cells that have been altered. Cells that came from *me*."

She raised her hand to her heart. "Me? No!"

"You wouldn't do that for your son?" He taunted, "Sssacrifice?"

"You're mad? I'm, I'm all he has left. Who would-"

"Kapo," Mr. Mortimer said, with the utmost contempt. "Just like your grandfather, Saul." Mr. Mortimer walked toward the living room. "Close all the windows and turn off the lights. We don't need the detective out front coming in, or anyone else."

"She's here?"

There was a sound of relief in Esther's tone.

She stepped closer to a wooden block of knives on the counter. "Then what are you doing if the police are here? Why can't you just find Dwight?" She reached for a cleaver.

He whispered to her mind, *The lights. NOW!*

"There's nothing in here but David's body and — oh, God." She flipped off the light in the kitchen, then the main switch in the living room.

In the darkness, Esther could hear a rustling of fabrics, then silence. The knife was ripped from her hand.

She gasped and stepped back, clutching herself.

"You'd be dead if I wanted you dead," he said in the darkness. "Genetically, it has to be close to mine."

"I don't understand," she said, unable to see where he was.

"Yitzhak Skinner. When my cells were still adapting to the genetic intruder I was infused with, I used my blood platelets to save your father-in-law from dying." Mr. Mortimer caught his breath. He continued to wheeze and fight for breath. "They combined with his own cellular structure and sustained me for what I had to do." Mr. Mortimer stopped again. "Like having a vaccine and antibodies at the same time. The Roma line is most compatible because many of those prisoners received the first trials. Their genes hold most of the altered DNA code. But not all. It's how you thought you'd survived the car accident. You have Saul's bloodline, but not enough to give you what I have. It's what you hope would help your son from the lab trials of Yitzhak. Because Yitzhak and I were the only ones who benefited from the serum before it was destroyed by the Russian attack when they liberated us."

"I wanted to see if it would work on my son."

"I was tempted myself today. It changes people. It'll change Dwight. He'll lose his innocence."

"He'll live."

"Not if I can't get to him. Forgive me." The sucking sound of muscle and tendons pulling away filled the room. Cartilage and bone snapped as Mr. Mortimer fed on Yitzhak's offspring. He stopped feasting and asked, "Did the Spiders come for me? Or just the boy?"

Esther couldn't answer while she listened to metal scraping and sawing deeply against what she could only imagine was bone. There was a *thud* and *crunch*, with more ripping and tearing and slurping. She covered her ears. Still, knowing what was happening, she soon got up.

"I can't do this. I can't be here for this. This is too much."

"Me or the boy?" Mr. Mortimer asked again, louder this time.

"Dwight. I'm sorry, but you were the price," she confessed and hurried to the kitchen.

He said nothing at first, then added, "Fool. The price was Dwight."

Taking a moment, she re-emerged. "They said they would cure him. From his birth defects...and the brain injury."

The cutting and skinning stopped.

"He wasn't pure," Mr. Mortimer said in a moment of revelation. "Hmm... Yitzhak wasn't completely Roma after all. His mother must have been a Jew. Interesting. It's why your son could have a genetic deficiency. Your sister. She most likely died because she was decapitated or her head was crushed in the accident. You knew this already...because you worked with Yitzhak and had the book, but it was incomplete. It caused the abnormalities. You traded me thinking the Spider could fix it, which means they have a book of their own, re-engineered new sciences, or they lied to you to get to the names." Mr. Mortimer cackled a laugh of ironic amusement, then crunched David's femur. The break and splintering sounds followed as Mr. Mortimer tore to the marrow. He chewed out loud with smaller crunches and bites as he did what he was created to do.

"I know where they could be," said Esther.

"I've just been waiting for you to say it. Go outside and ensure no one's watching if we leave from the back."

"What will you do?"

"Gorge."

Chapter Thirty-Three

Esther drove down the highway in the minivan. A pile of soccer balls and boxes in the trunk blocked the rear window, making it difficult for her to see if anyone was following them. Mr. Mortimer's burned flesh didn't smell quite so bad now, but she kept the windows cracked as they whisked through the fresh night air, dark corporate buildings rolling past.

Mr. Mortimer remained still for most of the ride to conserve energy. Living stem cells from David's bone marrow replaced and proliferated the dead and damaged with an ingested hematopoietic transplant. Parts of the charring were flaking away. Between the long shadows of the night along the highway, Esther could see new pink skin.

At long last, he spoke. "I'm not sure what is worse for your police friend. Losing a body or having a car stolen from the same street they are parked on.

"Are you...better?" Esther asked. "I've done genetic work and still can't wrap my head around this phenomenon."

"The phenomenon you speak of was genocide. This ability comes from over two hundred thousand dead. Even so, it continues. I've accomplished nothing in my lifelong slavery."

Esther said nothing more until they neared the location. "The facility is just up ahead," she said, pointing to an upcoming mid-sized and modest building. The structure was dated and drab compared to the other corporate neighbors in the office park that lined the frontage road parallel to the expressway. It fit the description of hiding in plain sight.

A handful of vehicles were parked in the dimly lit laboratory lot.

"Drive past the building," Mr. Mortimer suggested.

"Why aren't we turning in?"

"Turn in here and park," he said. "Lights off now."

Esther extinguished the Dodge's headlamps and turned into the adjacent office lot.

"Cameras," he pointed. "Drive through the vacant lot. Circle around the upcoming building. Turn here to the rear delivery drive. Now turn up here."

"Do you even know where you're having me go? This isn't the main research building." Esther looked back at the first laboratory, which she knew to be where the family had worked.

"Your son is not there. He's here." Mr. Mortimer pointed to another non-descript facility.

"How could you possibly know?"

"I can feel him. I can hear him. Can't you?"

Esther shook her head and wheezed. "No."

"You're Roma. The whisper isn't a trick or power. It's a oneness. Awareness of nature. Of surroundings. Connectiveness to family. To people. The universe."

"Well, I can't, so now what?"

"If I do not return within the next thirty minutes, do not follow. Call your detective. On your phone. Not your head."

Esther unfastened her seat belt. "I'm going with you."

"You'll be a liability. There are no doubt armed guards inside I will have to avoid or eliminate."

"How? You don't even have a gun. Do you?"

"I *am* everything I need."

D wight lay silent, staring through the tears that had long filled his eyes, up to the flickering fluorescent tube lighting that lined the water-stained ceiling above him. His arms were outstretched and restrained by black nylon straps wrapped around his feeble wrists that had lost most of their natural color, save for the redness that appeared with his intermittent struggles.

The tubes that surrounded him consisted of a ventilator snaked down his throat, a catheter that ran between his legs to a urine-filled bag hung on the gurney edge. A drip IV hung at his side and infused a vein under the white tape that secured the injection, and one pulling colors of red and pale white that connected to a large, razor sharp 25-gauge needle the size of a meat thermometer penetrating deep through the tissue, cored within bone. Electronic wire probes were attached to his cheeks and temples, which led to a monitor flashing blips and rhythms that far exceeded the baseline indicator levels. The room was large but tight, with racks of equipment and glassware and bottles. There were computer servers and wiring panels and white boards and cages. In the cages lining the length of two walls were tranquilized animals. Dogs. Cats. Three monkeys. A pig. Four gurneys, all covering heaps the lengths of the six-foot tables.

A voice across the room said, "We're almost finished with the initial extractions, my boy." The man, a type you could pass a million times and never notice, was wearing a white lab coat. Dress pants. A collared shirt. Loafers. He continued to fiddle with dials and rattle bursts of text on a computer keyboard. He could be any neighborhood dad working late so he could leave the next day early to attend a child's band concert or student conferences. "I'm disappointed your pain readings are so high. We'd hoped your tolerance would be much greater. I fear this is a waste of my time."

Dwight writhed under the restraints in sheer agony. Words, even if he had a clear throat, were lost in the swelling of thoughts racing through his innocent mind. Well beyond panic and despair, he squeezed his eyelids tight and focused on the sparkles and explosive colors in his mind.

He called through the ether one final time, *Monster.*

∾

The lights went dark. After a moment, they flickered as the backup generator engaged.

The geneticist looked to the ceiling, annoyed. "C'mon. I'm working," he said. Soon, the generator, too, ceased to power the facility, and a blanket of darkness fell.

Deft as a cat burglar, Mr. Mortimer took the easy way in. He gripped the casing of the rear entryway deadbolt, unscrewed it with a hard twist, and with a flick of his finger within the inter-working lowered the metal security bar, without a sound.

Mr. Mortimer scanned the bustling hallways as guards, researchers, and the like probed in the darkness. The workers laughed at themselves while they bumped into one another and called out for anyone who smoked actual cigarettes anymore who may have a light. Some went directly to their mobile device flash-lights, but they'd soon regret what they saw.

It was the security guard closest to the old Gypsy who had a flashlight who panned a small radius. The guard called on a radio for a status update and instruction on whether to shepherd the staff out of the building or contain them within an area.

Mr. Mortimer had no need to listen for an answer. He pounced on the guard with one arm wrapped around the man to prevent him from reaching for a weapon. Mr. Mortimer's free hand hooked right onto the man's throat. Fingers clenched, he crushed the man's windpipe and dropped him to suffocate on the ground.

Taking the guard's firearm was an option, but silence and confusion were better than announcing a hostile presence with a gunshot, causing a convergence of other armed personnel.

The question of innocents wasn't necessary. To Mr. Mortimer, anyone and everyone in this facility was complicit. The Nuremberg Trials had failed to exact a toll on passive contributions to Nazi killings. There would be no such debate tonight.

As Mr. Mortimer traveled down the hallway, any person in his way found themselves surprised within the flicker and strobes of falling phones. In the darkness, they were ravaged by a terrific force that smashed their heads into the wall or yanked their skulls back, snapping their necks. Some felt an abrupt cataclysmic force thrust into their chest walls, only to have their spines yanked forward through shattered ribs.

One by one, they fell. Each victim was equally unaware of the death that advanced upon them, breaking bones and extinguishing life as Mr. Mortimer followed an internal compass, driving him toward the young boy calling in desperation.

I'm coming, my angel, Mortimer whispered.

~

"There, there. That wasn't so bad," the scientist said while patting Dwight's head, having removed the tracheal intubation tube.

The man crossed the room after next extracting a small sample from the collection. He placed a few drops of Dwight's fluid under an electron microscope, then slid the slide into a computerized light bed. Within moments, a series of readings populated the screen.

"Well." He paused and fiddled with more knobs. "You aren't so special after all. No need for me to do any cutting."

Dwight groaned. His throat was irritated. "I have. Super. Powers."

"I'm afraid you don't. You have neurological damage that appears to have had some moderate stem cell treatment at some point. I assume this was from your grandfather's primitive research. Shame on him. You have an extra chromosome. Not a surprise. But unfortunately for our purposes, not enough of the residual bloodline and activator placed in your ancestors. Pity. Now you are of no use beyond further experimentation and dissection. Thank you very much for your donation."

The scientist turned back to the genetic composition analysis. "Your mother wanted us to fix you. To make you normal." He shrugged his shoulders in a moment of indifference, as if he were offered the choice of a ham or turkey sandwich. "Let's see what happens. I'll give you your superpowers."

Dwight cracked a weak but hopeful smile. "And then. I can fly. Away."

"No. I'm sorry, that won't happen. You can die. Right here. But afterward, I can open your skull and do a useful autopsy after we see how the treatment works on someone with your...afflictions." The man cracked a tight-lipped grin. "If you like animals, perhaps you know of a hippo that kills an old alpha's offspring. They do this for two primary reasons." The man crossed the room to a small white refrigerator, much like college students keep in their dorms. Unlike those of the co-eds keeping beers, seltzers, and sodas, his contained vials of crimson red life.

"First, because the hippo offspring carry genes of the former lead bull. A new bull doesn't want that gene line to continue. They root out all those offspring and kill them to ensure a new purity of stronger lines. Similarly, mothers who only want to care for their suckling are not ready to mate and produce new stronger offspring. This is why we do genetic research here and encourage others to submit DNA to learn of their lineage, which in reality is to kill off the weak suckling members of society. They get a nice family tree, while we can track superior genetic samples, like mortality, health, and fertility. We sell that data to our dating apps and matchmaking services. We can then develop viruses, bacteria, and other biological weapons to control that population. To reduce the herd. Root out the weak. The old. The feeble. Feeble children like you. It has been very successful in Iceland, where the population does what is best by testing before birth. It eliminates burdens."

He injected a long syringe into the rubber cap and drew a full dose of the genetically altered mix of embryonic and adult stem cell blood.

Dwight's eyes followed the man as he approached.

"You don't like needles very much, do you?"

The boy shook his head.

"I should think not." The man admired the medieval-looking dispenser and its long, blunt end 16-gauge needle. "But I don't see anyone else in the room to tell me otherwise."

"He's here. For me."

"And who would that be?" The man turned his head around the room, mocking the suggestion. "No one's here for you. No one wants to be here for you, which is why you are here. Modern-day infanticide and genetic deselection by disease and food additives are so much less messy than the works of our predecessors. You do not differ from other weak mammals. Chimpanzees, dolphins, lions, and bears all do the same. Why should we do anything less? At least we'll see if you can be corrected. The beauty of science." He twisted Dwight's head and plunged the steel deep into the child's neck base. He discharged the platelet-rich injection into one spot, then another.

Dwight shrieked under the shock of the intense pain.

The doctor pulled at Dwight's head, then thrust the needle again up past the spine through a narrow opening to the brainstem.

As he extracted the bloodstained needle and moved to another injection site, a viselike set of fingers clawed over his hand and flicked over with a twist, breaking the device from the man's wrist.

"Who the. . . ?"

Chapter Thirty-Four

M r. Mortimer hammered the heavy duty medical injection device into the scientist's skull and shot a rigid thumb into the man's throat, crushing his larynx. The scientist collapsed into a lifeless heap. Mr. Mortimer hurried to Dwight's side and found him moderately conscious.

"You came," Dwight moaned. "What happened to your body?"

Mr. Mortimer set out to free the young boy from the cords, wires, pumps, and straps. Innovations of extermination. "I got a little injured. And yes, this time it hurt."

"Can we go home?"

"Yes, I'm taking you home."

"Are there more bad people here?"

"Yes, Dwight. I'm afraid there are. When we leave, I need you to tell me who is dark and who is light. I need you to trust your heart, not your eyes. We want to make sure no innocent police have come. Can you do that for me?"

"I'm sleepy. I feel different. It burns."

"It's okay."

Mr. Mortimer noted the blood that had been drained from

Dwight. He was too weak to move. A reversal from extraction to transfusion would work, but it would take time.

The remaining serum lay tempting on the cart.

Dwight followed Mr. Mortimer's stare. "Is that more super-power medicine?" Dwight asked, without a hitch.

"Yes. It's cell replacement. It will change you more. You don't want that. You have enough powers, Dwight. You are more magical than any young boy I have ever met. Your power to see people for who they are, and hold hope for who they are not, is what I fear is missing in humanity. You're perfect. You are the true master race. One we can only aspire to."

"I'm different."

"We're all different." Mr. Mortimer grabbed the boy's hand. "And we're all the same."

Dwight's voice weakened with every remark. "I can't do things."

From Dwight's fluid speech pattern, Mr. Mortimer knew he was already changing. "You can do anything." He squeezed Dwight's hand.

Dwight's eyes rolled back into their sockets. "I can't do anything. No one likes me." His hand went limp. "Help me."

Mr. Mortimer rubbed at his own eyelids. His tear ducts had recovered, and tears streamed down his damaged face. "I love you, Dwight. Mr. Crumb Buckets, which is why I can't help you."

Esther charged into the room. "Oh, God. Is he?"

"I'm afraid he is dying. They injected him but removed a lot of his blood so the treatment would isolate in his brain."

"But you said...I thought..." She pawed at her head as she rushed to her son in hysterics. "What is all this? What did they do?"

Mr. Mortimer said nothing.

"Can't you do something? You're just going to stand there? You kill all these people to watch him die? Can't you give him your blood?"

Dwight's body began to convulse. He was choking from seizures.

"Do something! I know you must be able to do something. I know there's more you can do that you're not doing. I saw the research notes. Goddamnit, do something for him!"

"He's better dead."

"No. No. Don't say that. He wouldn't want that. He loves you. He trusts you. Save him. You said you loved him. Fix him. You have to be able to fix him." Esther looked around the room in desperation. "What is that?" she asked, eyeing the serum. "Is that it? Is that what they were going to give him?"

Mr. Mortimer stayed silent.

"Give it to him. Or this whole thing has been for nothing." She scrambled for the large syringe.

Mr. Mortimer stepped in front of Dwight. He grabbed Esther's arm as she rushed back, willing to try anything. "You don't know what you're saying."

She resisted and pounded on Mr. Mortimer's chest. "He's my son!"

"Not anymore."

"You goddamn monster." She tried to claw at his face, but he caught the hand. "I know where the book is. I know where David hid it."

Whether Mr. Mortimer sensed the truth or wanted it to be real, his obligation to protect the Romani forced him to consider the possibility. He took the device from Esther's hand and plunged the serum into Dwight's upper arm. Unsure of what the entire amount would do to a child, he sent half the volume into Dwight's body, tossing the remainder in the syringe to the floor. He feeds the transfusion needle into Dwight's wrist to replenish his blood supply. *Miro dev.*

"If I wasn't already damned, I have now forsaken innocents of this world for certain."

From outside of the door, clamor grew in volume and voices.

"Can you carry him?" Mr. Mortimer asked.

"I'll try. What are you planning?"

"Killing Spiders," he replied. "The bag must empty before we can go. He can't leave yet."

Esther asked the inevitable. "And what if it doesn't finish soon?"

"Then I'll be back."

"You're leaving?" Concern grew in her voice. "What if they come before you return?"

"There will be no *they* left to come in," he said, exiting the room.

Esther closed her eyes and covered her ears to drown out the screams and pleas from beyond the walls. The acoustic horror show endured for minutes, only to be interrupted by cracks of gunfire before starting anew. And then it all fell silent, save for the soft moans of her son.

Esther eyed the remaining serum that had been discarded on the floor. She stood and walked toward it.

Chapter Thirty-Five

M r. Mortimer was not quite at full strength. Still, he was able to make short work of the men who'd learned of the intruder. None could imagine what they'd seen in the flashes of gunfire light. In death, they would remember nothing.

Mr. Mortimer navigated the dark hallways back to Dwight. He feared for what he would see in Dwight. As he approached the door, he heard a rapid patter behind him. The patter turned into a colossal blow.

Mr. Mortimer flew front first into the cinder block wall. A vise-like grip grabbed his head and slammed it into the formed concrete. Fists of iron pummeled his ribs until he fell to the ground. Defenseless, Mr. Mortimer rolled to his side to see his attacker.

The six-foot-four Austrian-born Waffen-SS officer, Otto Skorzeny, towered above Mr. Mortimer, looking as formidable as he was at Auschwitz with Klaus Barbie. The man nicknamed "Scarface" kicked Mr. Mortimer repeatedly.

"Zigeuner. You don't die so easily. You look like you were taken from an oven. How appropriate. We met nearly a century ago now. The imposter in the bandage. And now you're famous.

The great Mossad assassin. Taking vengeance for the dead. So moving, as I, too, work for Mossad. Well, this is your end. And then time to kill your little Untermensch Jew boy. Pitty, my militiamen were so looking forward to finding you and your people. They were so close to having some fun."

Mr. Mortimer tight lips broke to a sinister grin. *Jekh dilo kerel but dile hai but dile keren dilimata. Na bister. Opre Roma!* Mr. Mortimer touched his own temples as he chanted.

Skorzeny stumbled backward, clutching his own head.

The voice channeled through Mr. Mortimer screamed; a shrill scream, followed by more of the forgotten words of the most ancient nomadic blood lines.

Skorzeny pleaded in agony, begging Mr. Mortimer to stop.

The tongues continued with words going further back in time. *Maa Kali*, Mr. Mortimer prayed to the Dark Mother, *Om MahaKalyai, Ca VidmaheSmasanaVasinyai, Ca DhimahiTanno Kali Prachodayat. Om Sri Maha Kalikayai Namah.*

A brilliance of light formed around Mr. Mortimer. First red, then orange, a blinding yellow, then white.

Skorzeny shrieked. Blinded, his eyes bled. They burned in the presence of sacred Sanskrit utterances.

Mr. Mortimer's burned flesh fell from his body. The flakes of dark ash turned to fine dust as they hit the ground. Rejuvenated and strong, Mr. Mortimer raised his leg over Otto Skorzeny and grit his teeth in rage.

The whimpering man could do nothing.

"Enough hate."

Chapter Thirty-Six

When Mr. Mortimer entered the room, he saw Dwight had returned to the living. He was alert and calm, as was his mother.

So, too, was Mr. Mortimer. Standing before them in the doorway, he was a changed man. A man who could have passed for someone in his mid-forties. Barely clothed, his body appeared solid. Whole. His breathing was measured, and he didn't appear to have an ounce of fatigue. His former wounds were healed.

"We can leave. We'll have to move fast. More men will come soon, and if they don't find us here, they'll come looking for us. We'll need to go for help."

Shocked at the transformed monster to a much younger version of himself, his voice unchanged but stronger, Esther could only muster the words, "Police?"

Mr. Mortimer smirked. "Not the police. Our people. They are about an hour's drive from here. Follow me and keep your eyes only on my back. Do you understand, Dwight?"

"I can look. I'm old enough to see." Dwight said, with confidence and clarity of speech. "Mom, hold my hand. Keep your eyes closed."

Esther swallowed hard. "Dwight?"

Chapter Thirty-Seven

Two days later:
Illinois/Wisconsin Border
Private campground

The middle-aged Romani bandolier chief addressed, with outstretched arms, the alliance of households gathered around the fire.

"We have come together as such a small representation of the *natsia*. This nation of our *kampaniyia* has not been gathered at this hour to settle a dispute, but rather a request. And so, men and women alike must be present to share their voice of support or concern before that request can be considered further."

Members of the assembled clan leaderships mumbled among their *familia* as they sat together in small and large pods of men, women, and children.

The leader of the *Kris* proceedings continued. "You have been invited from afar because of your authority, and because many of you have benefited from Mortimer the Undead's gifts to you all. He is blood family to all of our camps. He has given yet never taken."

The fire flickered and sparked. Shadows and light danced

with one another across the Romani faces. The campsite was filled with white RVs, small and large. Intricate and modest. The scene was a Burning Man event meets a KOA campground kumbaya folk gathering with some leftover game day tailgaters. The group was diverse yet the same. Unique but joined. It was family.

"There is a matter of justice at hand. One that we may decide we must wash our hands of. And yet, as we wish for our behavior to remain pure, the pollution of hate toward our people remains and has reared its head and evil eye toward Roma everywhere."

A voice from the crowd boomed, "The *gaje* will always think of us as thieves. What fool here expects us to rise up or cast chaos? It will be an end to us all."

Another called out, "We do not go to war without provocation. There is nothing we have not seen before. Nothing we will not see again."

The rumblings of agreement sounded like the pounding of horse hooves on hard ground.

Mortimer stood. Esther remained in the shadows of the gathering, Dwight still in the car, sleeping to recover. "Your families died at their hands," he said. "The fascists of the Reich are here. Here for me. Here for you. They have your names. They know your bloodline. It is why you continue to move. The Nazis have never stopped, and never will. You are the Nazi gold. The secret to their future."

The crowd hushed save for one voice. "You call the fat, tattooed boys marching in the suburbs with flags and helmets a threat? They go home as soon as their mothers call them to clean their room."

The gatherers laughed in unison.

Mortimer removed his glasses. Some had witnessed the pitch of his eyes before. Others had only heard of the cursed witchery that had befallen him. His secret was safe among his people. "Our laws do not permit the taking of a life. That does not mean we cannot defend ourselves. This is an ancient and enduring evil that seeks to destroy our kind. It is why I break our laws. And why I, alone, have borne this burden."

An old woman they called *Duda*, who Esther had met that morning, caught her gaze. The woman whispered, *Esther, queen of Persia. Who saved her people from genocide. Astra. Strix to our people across the waters. Striya in our Sanskrit ways. The succubus. The one who kills babies out of jealousy and spite. I see the evil in you.*

Esther turned away. The men bantered on, oblivious to the enshrouding in their midst.

"What can they want with us?" a middle-aged member asked. "Our numbers are few. We remain in hiding save for some ghettos across the globe. These are modern times. Box cars and camps are not a threat. Nothing can be changed except our exposure if we get involved. We continue to raise awareness through our peace, politics, and community giving."

The murmurs and rumblings grew again.

Mr. Mortimer spoke. "Your parents. Perhaps grandparents, for some, were all given regular injections in the camps. It wasn't all for sterilization. There was a reason we were the preferred people to be selected for experiments. Not that we were expendable. We were the true Aryans. Those who survived were spared for a reason. You have heard of the Nazi gold smuggled out of Germany."

"And diamonds that you have brought us," a voice heralded from around the fire.

The crowd laughed.

"Yes, let's find the gold," another member exclaimed. "That is a mission I will join."

"*You* are the gold!" Mortimer shouted. The gold runs through your veins. Your DNA that has traveled from ages ago in India is one of the purist races. And they have isolated a gene that remains dormant in our lineage they primed with their experiments. One we couldn't know exists, that they now wish to collect. And soon, when that is exposed, *you* will be collected again. Imagine what it will be like the next time. Of all the prisoners and Family Camp stories, ours were the worst. Ankle-deep mud, no new clothes, unusable latrines. A complete liquidation of anyone who stepped into the infirmary. You will be murdered again."

The camp erupted in argument. Voices of reason, rationality, and dissent battled from the Roma seated in plastic lawn chairs.

The *Kris* leader was unsuccessful. Mortimer was unsuccessful.

The elderly whispering woman from the back came forward to the fire. She lifted her long dress up to her neck, exposing her nakedness to the group in an old and rarely used custom of skirt-tossing to halt the argument.

Holding attention and power, the woman dropped the cloth from her fingertips, exposing a long ceremonial knife. She unsheathed the decorated blade, turning for all to see, and drew the sharpness across her faded camp tattoo until blood flowed. She licked the steel and returned it to its cover before handing it to Mortimer.

"A great evil has returned," she said, with an eye directed to Esther. "I give you my four grandsons. I give you my blood for the blood they have taken. For the blood intended to be spilled."

"This is nonsense," a voice countered from the darkness. "This is no credible threat. Show me proof. Give us a sign. Show us what we are really fighting for, and what is truly at stake."

Despite being warned to stay in the vehicle, Dwight dashed by Esther and then past Mr. Mortimer. He ran to the fire. In the span of a blink, he was at the center of the clan members' meeting, staring in wonderment at the bright colors emanating from the group's energy. Colors that bore no black. Dwight basked in the warmth of the auras that radiated a greater comfort and heat than the flickering flames themselves.

He raised his head, removed the mask and snorkel, and tossed them blindly into the fire. "I found your family, Zayde."

Then Dwight danced just as he had danced with Mr. Mortimer only days ago. He danced the dance of the Romani. From his mouth came the unhindered, melodic lyrics of the

Gypsy soul. How the words found his tongue was a mystery to even Mortimer, who had not heard the songs since life in the Auschwitz family camp over seventy-five years prior. From the darkness in the stead of dissent came a violin that drifted in to accompany the small cherubic voice.

"We kill the murderers," Dwight said. "Just as they killed our people. They should bleed like they spilled our blood."

The Romani before him soon knew the answer. The matter was settled. It was time to sing and dance as the generations before them had, even while locked away, starving and diseased with feelings of isolation and despair. The world could take their lives, but no one could take their ancient way.

Mortimer eyed Dwight with a newfound concern, and the change overtaking him.

Esther rubbed her clammy hands down her sides.

Chapter Thirty-Eight

What soldiers call "Oh-dark-thirty," the deepest and darkest time of the night to attack, the Roma had found to be the safest time, to travel to avoid confrontation and the dangers of harassment between towns. Hence, what the Jews called *kismet* was the destiny these two groups should face off.

Mortimer sat on his wraparound front porch, sipping bourbon and humming, when the vehicle lights snaked through the neighborhood. He counted six in total before the drivers turned off the headlamps. A simple sum was six vehicles, four to five men in each meant up to thirty men. He felt at his core the heat of hate and fear spilling closer.

From Mr. Mortimer's experience, four to five men would pour in the entrances to the front, side, and rear, while the rest would closely follow, leaving a handful waiting around the outside.

The old man puffed on his cigar. The coal grew hot. The glow cast enough light on his face that anyone looking for him would find their target. The vehicles sped up as he tossed the Dominican hand-rolled tobacco off the porch onto the long burning logs in his fire pit.

"And the monster declared, the entire village was roused to attack with stones and missile weapons, but I will not take refuge in fear," he quoted while walking into the house. *They are here*, he whispered. "Arbeit macht frei."

Whereas the Black Order of Nazi Germany were elite trained commandos, these hate-filled men had played soldiers in the Midwest forests and farm fields while nourishing their souls on racist and anti-Semitic ideas. Hailing from their mother's basement sofas to finding brotherhood around militia bonfires, these conspiracy-minded extremists hoped to kill or capture the "Jew-loving Nazi traitor" their commander, Otto, had rallied them to attack.

The Black Order Spiders scurried from their caravan. Black dots of armed men swarmed Mr. Mortimer's property in the quiet night. They spread across the home, seeing vulnerable breaching points, just as the Gypsy predicted.

Preparing to kick in the door, the first squad found the door unlocked. With a turn of the knob, the men entered behind the squeak of the hinges and huffing breaths. Their footfalls creaked as they crept through the barren domicile. Spreading out to the array of closed doors, each man turned a knob, only to be met with yet another dark, empty room.

In a simultaneous effort, the blades of the Roma's found their marks in slashes, thrusts, and deep evisceration.

The Spiders screamed in terror and pain. Those who found their throats slashed only wheezed through the gurgle of choking blood.

The second team of breachers heard the horror through the thin walls. They rushed to the scene, clamoring through the narrow entryway, only to be met by the same fate from the front and back. The quick blades made short and quiet work of the ill-prepared assaulters. They fell in pools of their own blood, writing about themselves, grabbing one another in agony, fear, and utter panic.

Other men now dashed about in confusion. They shouted and called out each other's names. White lights were activated from their accessorized weapons. They strobed throughout the room, seeking an enemy not yet visible.

A door burst open.

The Spiders panicked and directed all fire to the surprising noise. Bullets ripped through their fellow men in frantic fratricide. Spent ammunition casings chimed like melodic hail as they bounced off the hardwood floors.

"Spread out. He's in here somewhere."

"How can he be everywhere?"

A man shouted, "I found a staircase!" He rushed down the steps.

A loud scream came from the darkness, then trailed off to a series of small whimpers before going silent.

"Get down there!"

No one moved.

The final team in the house had come through the front entry and dashed up the tiered staircase after spotting a figure fleeing. At the second floor landing, they were greeted by a long hallway lined with closed doors. The men slowed their paces and filed down the corridor, not knowing where to start.

Were it not for the darkness, each Spider would have recognized a similar blank look written across the others' faces. The house was filled with screams and shouts emitting from below their feet.

"He must have gotten downstairs," a man said.

"Let's head back."

The surrounding doors opened in unison.

Hands and blades lashed out.

When the remaining men on the outside heard the cries and pleas for help, they rushed into the death mill.

They met the same fate as warm steel ripped through their bodies and knife butts and hilts crushed into their skulls.

Otto Skorzeny remained by the vehicles. He'd sent his men into battle but remained warry from what he'd experienced in the lab.

Tired of words and the fight, Mr. Mortimer heaved an axe from his woodpile, striking Otto in the back of the neck. Skorzeny's head rolled on the grass, a look of surprise frozen on his face.

Mr. Mortimer stepped over the corpse without a sound. He and his compatriots walked among the writhing hate group, kicking weapons from their hands.

Those on the ground who could still talk spouted insults and idle threats. The Roma remained silent and exited the carnage.

They walked in measured, unhurried steps down the porch steps. Each took a burning log in hand and flung them through the doorways and glass windows. A couple of men gathered the headless body of Skorzeny and tossed it in the fire.

Mr. Mortimer watched the blaze, and his Roma family slipped into the shadows and returned to their near and far away camps. He held the lifeless head of Skorzeny in his hands and fled before the Skokie Police and Fire Department made their near-nightly call to this once quiet neighborhood. Skorzeny would be excellent nourishment.

Chapter Thirty-Nine

Walking along the neighborhood's shadows and coverings, Mr. Mortimer gave a light rap on the Skinners' back door. In moments, the amber kitchen light switched on.

Esther greeted him, dressed with trepidation and a long dark robe. "What happened?"

Mr. Mortimer stood silent in the open doorway. He cocked his head.

The red, white, and blue lights of emergency response vehicles cast prismatic flashes through homes and to the treetops. Some flickers swirled in the kitchen as they spoke, having stolen entry from the front door's upper window glass.

"I didn't expect you so soon. I mean, I heard the sirens. Are you okay? Did your people come to help?"

"*My* people?" Mr. Mortimer walked through the kitchen, Esther trailing close behind.

"If you're looking for Dwight, he's asleep. Still recovering. He was exhausted. I was just upstairs with him."

"May I see him?"

"He's asleep."

Mr. Mortimer brushed past Esther, climbed the stairs, and

turned to the closed door of Dwight. "I'll be leaving soon. I'd like to say goodbye to him. Properly." Mr. Mortimer turned the knob.

"I really don't have the books. Sorry."

Mr. Mortimer turned. "Disappointing," he said, then continued to see Dwight.

"David couldn't handle the pressure. He couldn't imagine having the papers of that crazy Nazi doctor," she justified.

"Mengele. It was the burden David carried. He knew he was to be the next keeper. A small price for him to pay compared to those before him."

"No," she protested. "David read the books. The notes. Even without his father telling him, he knew he was to be the one who fed you through a lifetime of transfusions. It's why we all lived in isolation. Why he needed a strong son. Your legacy created his madness. They could have burned the stupid books. Then no one would know. Could have let you die. What purpose *do* you serve?"

"If there were other records, we needed these to find and protect the Roma from the camps first. To learn who would be taken next. Executed."

"You and Yitzhak are so stupid. So old. They have goddamn databases of names open to the public. I could have had another son. David wouldn't listen. He didn't want the burden. I thought he was talking about Dwight. My mother-in-law thought it was about Dwight. It was about you. You were the burden."

Mr. Mortimer opened the door to Dwight's room.

The boy lunged from the darkness with a large kitchen knife. He speared the old Romani in the gut, pulled out the knife, and struck again and again. "I have the powers now!" Dwight yelled. "All the powers. And the stupid *old-Dwight* and his colors are dead."

Mr. Mortimer fell to the ground, grasping at his wounds, unwilling to respond.

Esther retrieved a small revolver from her robe. "I told him how I killed his brother and father to protect him from you and those gypsy vagabonds."

From the kitchen stepped Detective Jefferson. "Put the gun down, Mrs. Skinner." She, too, had her 9mm Hellcat pistol drawn from the shoulder holster. The detective froze upon seeing Dwight at the top of the stairs, bloodied knife in his hand, and what looked to be...a younger Mr. Mortimer?

She managed to muster in a calming voice, "You, too, Dwight. Please put the knife down."

"No," Dwight refused.

"C'mon Dwight, I'm your friend. Remember? The yellow lady?"

"You're not yellow. You're black. I'm not your friend."

Esther twisted to the detective, seizing the moment, gun raised with a finger on the trigger.

Detective Jefferson fired three shots in succession, hitting Esther center mass.

Esther's body hiccupped with each hollow point round thumping her body. She collapsed, dropping the weapon, the impact wounds leaking and spreading through the fabric of her clothes.

Dwight, watching his mother collapse, lowered his knife for a moment, then sprung to charge down the stairs at Detective Jefferson.

Mr. Mortimer rose.

He grabbed Dwight, who slashed and cut anything in his field of view.

Mr. Mortimer tried to parry the attack. With a hammering blow, he knocked the knife out of Dwight's firm grasp.

He lunged for the boy, wrapping Dwight in a bear hug, and was able to grab Dwight's head. *It should never have been, sweet boy.*

Dwight writhed to escape. He reached back, clawing and screaming in rage.

Mr. Mortimer gave a quick, snapping twist.

Stunned at the cascading events, the detective was slow to turn her weapon on Mr. Mortimer. She fired until Mr. Mortimer wilted lifeless upon Dwight.

"Mother of God," Detective Jefferson said, holstering her weapon. She stomped her feet and fisted her head. She turned herself around and around in a circle, trying to make sense. "What did you people just do?" she kept repeating. "What did you make me do? Oh, my God."

In afterthought, she leapt to the bodies. Checked for any signs of life. Dwight had no pulse. His breath, gone. The heartbeats of Mr. Mortimer and Esther were faint and slow but existent. Her eyes dropped to the Auschwitz tattoo on Mr. Mortimer's arm.

"How do you look like you do? How did you change? What happened to that dear, sweet boy?" Detective Jefferson screamed a banshee's cry of pain and confusion. Of helplessness as she rushed for the door to get help.

The Skinner family nearly all gone, Esther gasped a loud, guttural, wheezing attempt for more air.

Chapter Forty

"Shots fired! Shots fired! I need help! Medical evacuation requested immediately!" Detective Jefferson screamed out the door toward the emergency vehicles parked up and down the neighborhood street. She raced toward the lights.

A police officer encouraging neighbors to stay back was the first to see the detective running in his direction.

"I have two GSWs down. One unresponsive with a broken neck. I need an EMT."

The officer radioed to all open channels and directed Detective Jefferson back to the house.

"She's trying to breathe. I had to take the shot," she repeated as they ran. "And then he just killed the boy. But the boy stabbed him. I had to. Oh, my God, oh, my God." She stopped at the front steps and flapped her arms and hands. She took deep breaths in and out. "The old man was supposed to be dead. That entire house is filled...with dead people. And the pieces...of her husband?" She panted. "What in God's name did they do?"

Putting his arm around the frantic detective, he said as he squeezed her, "You're okay. Did what you had to. Try to calm down. Let me get inside and help them." He broke the contact to go assess.

Detective Jefferson nearly collapsed on the stoop. The tears rained freely. She pounded her legs before burying her face in her hands.

"Detective," the officer called from inside.

Jefferson wiped her eyes. It was futile as she thought of her first meeting with Dwight and his mask and snorkel. "I'm coming," she said, with a sniff. "I'm coming. Oh, God. That poor little boy."

"Oh, God," she heard from the entryway. "I can't," the police officer said as he burst through the door frame and vomited down the stairs. He shook his head and continued to purge his stomach uncontrollably.

Detective Jefferson peered into the home. She opened the door wider to get a better look, then stepped back inside.

Dark red, the most noticeable angry color throughout the home, had fully seeped into the carpet and between the hard wood planks.

A diminishing trail of blood stained the floor in a series of drizzles and drops that led from the stairs to the hallway, past the kitchen, to the back door.

The simple hanging kitchen table sconce flickered. Shadows danced in its dirty amber rhythm.

A slight sound of thunder rumbled in the distance between the wails of sirens.

There was no more noise, chaos, secrets, or lies in the Skinners' house.

Esther and Dwight lay in their own lifeless pools. Their heads and Mr. Mortimer gone.

Chapter Forty-One

Skokie Lagoons

The campfire crackled to the audience of one. Holding Esther's bodiless head in his hands, her flesh all but eaten, Mr. Mortimer sat cross-legged on the cold forest floor. Fallen leaves swirled around him as the autumn winds grew. The flame's radiance in the pitch of night shone dark trails of tears that flowed from the eyelid pits of the broken Romani, once called Nehemia. A name he hadn't heard in over 75-five years.

Mr. Mortimer's black eyes filled and dripped from his high cheekbones. "In truth," he confessed, "I have been called a monster in my past. Considered one long before that..." He bit and chewed. "In war, men become monsters when their fear is vanquished after the first bloodletting on the battlefield...in fact, we called ourselves monsters, of sorts, when we became the German's conscripts. Felt their power until it came back to roost." He sighed and wiped his mouth. Then his cheek. "I wonder, because of this, Esther, and the words of your dear boy now. A boy cursed since birth with the affliction beyond mental slowness. A meaningless child at the time, who may have been better off dying upon leaving your womb. A nothing to me, who called me a monster. Or so I once thought." He looked down. Dark shadows and a few passing leaves covered Dwight's head, which was also draped by a blood-soaked canvas bag before Mr. Mortimer's spread knees. "What did he know of monstrosity without looking at his own future reflection, and those around him? What I knew. Did he not know what his fate would hold as a monster in his own right? And still his words impaled my soul in a manner I have not felt since nearly a lifetime ago, when I said goodbye to Esmeralda. And to my young Django..." Mr. Mortimer whimpered a painful, wordless cry of suffering in the silence of the woods and adjudicator of the night's sky. "A morning I've cast so far away from memory, I no longer hold it as my own. How could I have been such a monster to leave — and for what? I can no longer smell her hair. Or remember her sweet voice. And to my own son...I can't recall the sound of his small voice. Yet if I should hear it tomorrow, which I concede is ridiculous, I would know it in an instant...I would as quickly be reduced to tears and drawn to my knees. To beg forgiveness from them both..."

He placed Esther's head in the glowing fire. Embers jumped in delight as they consumed her hair with a rush of little crackles and spark.

"How, then, could I make your boy see me not for what I am, for what I have been, but for what I covet? In truth, he may have been the purest being I have ever met. I knew in an instant I loved him, and I wanted him to love me back. And he did.

"I no longer want to be the monster I am and fear I will always be. I want to know love and be loved. So much hate. Forgive me for what I never intended to become." He uncovered Dwight's head, gave it a kiss on the forehead, and lowered it, too, to the dancing flames.

Mr. Mortimer smiled as he saw the bright colors rise. "I'll see you soon, too, Dwight. But first, I have to protect our people. I need to help Rabbi Moshe protect his. I need to help the detective find the killers she is so passionate about. Good bye for now. Much work to be done."

Epilogue

Yitzhak Skinner awoke. He gasped for breath and sought for sight that still never came in the perpetual darkness of his cramped tomb. Trapped six feet below the surface, he clawed in his casket with the few moments of life he had. He tore at the shredded coffin lining, as he had during each damning rebirth. Yitzhak's ripped fingernails hung from the splintering wood fibers cleaved from his flesh in hysterical desperation. Regeneration had occurred for weeks, but with no air, food, or water, he succumbed to death again and again, stolen from his eternal sleep.

In the minutes of life afforded between the perpetual death throes, he silently screamed and scratched in the nothingness of his eventual demise.

With no nourishment to feed his blood cells, short of a rotting piece of fruit stuck deep within his trachea, the old man's life-system, sustained by imperfect regenerative engineering by his own redesign, failed time and again. The grapes of wrath were victorious.

Laying atop the journals David buried him over, Yitzhak occasionally whispered in the mere seconds to spare, hoping someone, somewhere would hear.

After Dwight's own silence, the outcome remained the same from the one he knew.

Go back to sleep, my dear rabbit, Mr. Mortimer would reply. *The secrets must remain safe.*

The End

Acknowledgments

The subjects within this writing and their depths required both knowledge and sensitivity. It required extensive research and reach-outs to the diverse groups portrayed, for both feedback and ideas. I thank my wife, Shilpa, and daughters, Sedona and Aiyana, for instilling in me greater sensitivity and awareness over the years that helped in that understanding. My son, Braeden, for asking me to write him a story of a differently abled boy who gets kidnapped and that would be appropriate for him to read. Sorry it took so long, buddy.

Specific to this novel, in addition to those who wished to remain anonymous, I benefited from the knowledge, skills, and advice of five editors with varying backgrounds who answered my endless questions and validated voice, subject matter, and word choices. Thank you to Eve Porinchak, Amy Scott, Rebecca Klassen, Lyndsey "Horror-"Smith, and Karen Boston, who all took me from various phases of editorial developmental to copy suggestions.

Thank you to Michael Picco, one of my favorite horror writers, who was an early beta reader and provided excellent additional feedback to amp things up. Author John Baltisberger's horror expertise with Jewish elements, and Josh Schlossberg, from Denver Horror Collective's The Jewish Book of Horror, were especially helpful in navigating some cultural nuances.

And always, thanks to my go-to beta reader, Bodo Pfundl who writes better English than me and who helped with German phrases and words.

Meet the Author

Prior to becoming an author, J.T. Patten worked for the government intelligence and military special operations community. He was a subject matter authority on Iran and the Islamic Revolutionary Guard Corps (IRGC), Qods Force, Irregular and Unconventional Warfare strategies in counterterrorism, intelligence collection, and social network disruption. Primary funtions included supporting operational elements of the IC; analytical and mission support and instructor to SOCOM J2, 2X, 25, 35, 3X, JSOC, DIA; concept design for TSWG; advisor and trainer to United States Army Special Operations Command G-3X, Sensitive Activities Division; and various TSOCs.

Learn more about J.T. at:
https://jtpattenbooks.com/bio

Made in United States
North Haven, CT
28 November 2022

27449939R00131